FRIDAY AFTERNOON

and Other Stories

T.D. JOHNSTON

Copyright © 2016 by T.D. Johnston

ISBN: 978-0-9882497-7-6
Library of Congress Control Number: 2016933536

Printed in the United States of America

Publisher: Battersea Books
Design: Tim Devine Design

FIRST EDITION

Requests for such permissions should be addressed to:

Battersea Books
221 Johnson Landing Road
Beaufort, SC 29907
Visit T.D. Johnston online at
www.tdjohnston.com

Advance Praise for

FRIDAY AFTERNOON

and Other Stories

"As he proves emphatically with his new collection, *Friday Afternoon and Other Stories*, T.D. Johnston is clearly one of the modern masters of the short story."—*James Dodson, Editor,* **O. Henry Magazine** *and* **PineStraw Magazine**

~

"The short story is a uniquely powerful form, and T.D. Johnston has harnessed that power to stunning effect. The prose of this collection paints like John Updike and boxes like Norman Mailer upon the page. If it's true that Raymond Carver's arrival revitalized the short story's place in American literature, then with this collection a torch has been passed to a new master of the form." —*James Goertel, author of* **Carry Each His Burden**

~

"This collection of short stories proves without doubt that T.D. Johnston is one of the finest voices of contemporary short fiction. These stories are filled with wit, pathos, and compassion. Johnston skillfully leads his readers through the sometimes murky moral landscape of life to which we all can relate. Always firmly in control of where he wants to take us, he never leaves us disappointed."—*Ray Morrison, author of* **In a World of Small Truths**

~

"This superb collection proves that true suspense derives from moral choices. T.D. Johnston is a mesmerizing storyteller." —*Martin McCaw, author, winner of the Global Short Story Prize*

~

"Storyteller T.D. Johnston is a closer. He knows the secret that some writers never learn – that a great story demands a great ending. Some of his endings are deliciously open – almost like new beginnings – while others are as shocking and final as a door slammed in your face. In story after tantalizing story, Johnston sends his variously-flawed characters wobbling down the brutal balance beam of human existence – building tension as they go – then sticks his landing like an Olympic gymnast. Only then do we realize we've been holding our breath... and sometimes holding back tears."— *Margaret Evans, Editor,* **Lowcountry Weekly**

∽

"T.D. Johnston boldly explores a wide range of both subject matter and genre, with masterful attention to the old-age elements of good writing."—*Pat Conroy, author of* **The Prince of Tides**

∽

"T.D. Johnston, champion and master of the short story, focuses his artful eye on the American experience in a way that reveals the many facets of our souls. "—*Eric M. Witchey, winner of multiple awards for short fiction*

∽

"Lucky is the person who holds this book, for the pages inside bubble with danger, excitement, compassion, and humanity. T.D. Johnston's fiction will undoubtedly change how a reader sees and thinks. A needed literary voice."—*Mathieu Cailler, author of* **Loss Angeles**

∽

"You come home from a day of no surprises, thinking you'll just relax with a hot drink and something amusing to read. But then you pick up a short story from T.D. Johnston instead and, almost immediately, you're knocked off balance. It's just an insistent little nudge at first, but the nudges get more and more insistent, along with the knot forming in your stomach. You never see the end that's coming because it sneaks in around a corner where you never thought to look. T.D. Johnston isn't just a master of suspense. He's a master of surprise." —*Susan Mary Dowd, author of* **The Yard**

∽

"This is an important collection. Powerful, provocative, and significant. To read a T.D. Johnston story is to plunge head first into the world of unforgettable characters, 3-D experiences, and stunning surprises."—*Marjorie Brody, award-winning author and Pushcart Prize nominee, author of the psychological suspense novel,* **Twisted**

∾

"There are unspoken tributes in these stories of T.D. Johnston: O. Henry and Ray Bradbury and John Cheever come satisfyingly to my mind. But these moving stories are all Johnston's own, in voice and style and innovation of the genre he has done so much to revive with his inspired Short Story America. From the intensely human, wise but challenged Stan in "A Game of Chess" to the speeding and slow-to-understand CEO in "Friday Afternoon," we're all here in this book. And we've got to feel, as happens with the best of short stories, that at the end we may be surprised, even shamed, but we've been instructed, too: the best fiction inspires and teaches. It changes us for the better."—*Gregg Cusick, author, winner of the Lorian Hemingway Prize for Short Fiction*

∾

"The stories in T.D. Johnston's *Friday Afternoon and Other Stories* showcase the author's compassionate attention to emotional details, the vigor of his storytelling, and the rich variety in his voices, style, and subject matter—all crackling with the tension between hope and despair." —*Paul Elwork, author of* **The Girl Who Would Speak for the Dead**

∾

"T.D. Johnston's collection feels at once classic and fresh. Each story is its own world, immediate and enjoyable. Through his work at Short Story America, he has invigorated a community of writers, and this collection is a wonderful testament to his own mastery of the short story form." —*Alex Myers, author of* **Revolutionary** *(Simon & Schuster).*

∾

"At the present historical moment, T.D. Johnston may be the short story's best friend. A scholar of the form and a dedicated anthologist, he is foremost a storyteller, and the short form is his specialty. Whether evoking the Civil War or a contemporary moment, his eye for the precise, essential detail grounds his characters' experience in dilemmas and settings a reader is pleased to enter. His perspective is ultimately warm and humane, and it settles gracefully on men, women, boys and girls, in an invigorating array of circumstances. His growing body of work is a heartening testimony to the medium of short fiction."—*Richard Hawley, author of* **The Headmaster's Papers**

～

"*Friday Afternoon and Other Stories* is an impressive debut. In this collection, Johnston channels masters of short form fiction such as Raymond Carver, Flannery O'Connor, and William Gay, while writing fully original stories in his own voice. Start with "The Errand," continue with "Friday Afternoon," and then enjoy the rest of the wild and satisfying ride." —*Evan Kuhlman, author of* **Wolf Boy** *and* **The Last Invisible Boy**

～

"*Friday Afternoon and Other Stories* lends great honor to an American literary tradition. Through lean, active prose, with no time to spare, we are driven straight to the heart of the matter. We're shown how damaged characters grapple with exterior pressures while clawing through the grim and gritty landscapes of their inner worlds, and who by doing so, teach us to become more compassionate creatures." –*Jodi Paloni, author of* **They Could Live with Themselves**

～

"Once, while in West Hollywood discussing a series, an entertainment lawyer lamented, 'You just don't see quality material being delivered by authors with the style of a Rod Serling or Richard Matheson anymore.' Well, thanks, T.D. Johnston, for putting that myth to rest. With this collection of well-crafted, powerful tales, Johnston provides satisfying hope to those of us who love excellent short stories." —*Mark Hunt, Film Producer and Grammy Nominee,* **Tom Dowd and The Language of Music**

～

"T.D. Johnston's compassion for his characters is compelling and crucial to understanding people much like ourselves. Unique in its look at cruelty in the guise of conformity to the rules of the workplace, home place or road, *Friday Afternoon and Other Stories* is a tour de force that will stay with you for a very long time." — *Warren Slesinger, award-winning author, poet, and retired senior editor of the University of South Carolina Press*

~

"Erudite doomsters be damned. *Friday Afternoon and Other Stories* is proof positive that the Southern Gothic tradition - and the short story as an art form - are still alive and kicking. Highly recommended." —*Rolli, author of **God's Autobio***

~

"This collection by T.D. Johnston settles the reader in a comfortable easy chair and then proceeds to prick him with electrifying barbs, pelt him with bizarre happenings, or turn time and place upside down. In some cases, such as the opening story, "The Errand," we stay within normal boundaries, with the protagonist's anxiety brilliantly rendered. The theme of finding purpose in life is a *leitmotif* throughout, whether in the eerie "Friday Afternoon," in which a narcissistic and arrogant CEO of a floor-covering company gets his comeuppance, or in "A Morning Along the Way," in which a black teenage girl selects a boy because he will escape their Southern town and go to college, an ambition she shares. There are also some satirical and unforgettable Orwellian stories ("The Closing" and "Sixth Period"), set in a future where college degrees are sold to the highest bidder ("The Closing") and, in "Sixth Period," the seven deadly sins have been reduced by Congress to six: greed has been deleted by law because it is deemed an attribute. "A Game of Chess," a particular favorite of mine, is a moving diary narrative of a janitor whose character gains inner strength by story's end. Johnston's characters are often familiar—either like us or someone we know—but each gains uniqueness through his versatile storytelling."— *Laury A. Egan, author of **Fog and Other Stories** and **Jenny Kidd***

~

TABLE OF CONTENTS

For my wife, Stacey,
and for Brooke, Taylor and Nick

But in the grey of the morning,
My mind becomes confused
Between the dead and the sleeping
And the road that I must choose.

The Moody Blues, "The Question"

THE ERRAND

Robert stared at the rack of magazines. The titles glazed as he considered whether to call. She'd said something bride magazine. Bride something magazine. She was adamant. *Get the bride something magazine first, then the stuff from the wine shop. Cabernet from the reds aisle, and a cold chardonnay from the cooler behind the cash register. Remember that,* she'd said, *because the white has to be cold by the time Jay and Linda arrive.*

Jay and Linda don't like to drop a cube in a warm glass of chardonnay. Not like last time. Remember that, Robert. And don't dilly-dally. Robert was sure he had it, except for the bride something magazine. Something bride.

The rack had six brides. All smiling. All in white. He'd have to call. No question about it. *Georgia Bride, Atlanta Bride, Bride 2016, Bride Beautiful, Bridal Fashion* and *Bride.* He was relieved that he could eliminate *Bride,* because she'd said something bride, bride something, but definitely something. Still, there were five. He briefly considered buying all five, but the balance in the checking account worried him, and the credit card was maxed. He'd have to call.

But it was raining and the cell phone was in the car, and Jay and Linda would be there at eight. She wanted him back soon enough to change his sweater because he wore it two weeks ago at Kara Mortensen's party, and Linda had been there even though Jay was out of town.

Yes, Jay was out of town, she'd said. Sometimes his work took him out of town, *but then again if it didn't he wouldn't be driving that Lexus, Robert.*

He could not bring back the wrong something bride. He considered asking the girl behind the counter which bride magazine was best, but she had both hands busy preparing her red hair for the barrette that stuck like a cigarette from the left side of her mouth. He would have to call, but it was raining harder than when he came in, and he'd parked the Subaru around the corner in front of the wine shop.

She wouldn't like it one bit if he came back with wet hair, especially if Jay and Linda were early and he couldn't change his sweater.

Robert decided to ask the girl behind the counter if he could please make a local call, but the sound of his name stopped him.

"Bobby? Bobby Canton?"

He turned to find an elderly man grinning at him. The man, easily in his seventies, stood crookedly as if it were painful to stand without movement. He brushed water from the left shoulder of his tan trenchcoat.

"You're Bobby Canton, aren't you?"

For a moment, the old man looked familiar, but eight o'clock loomed. She would not be pleased if Linda saw him in this sweater twice in a row.

"Yes?"

"My gosh, Bobby, what's it been? Thirteen years or so? You've really grown up, sure have."

"Excuse me, but I— Oh, my God. Mr. Burris?" It was definitely Mr. Burris, but she would never buy a yarn about running into one of his old teachers. No way.

The old man extended a weathered hand. Robert shook it, and was surprised by Mr. Burris's strength. He had to be seventy-five by now.

"You look wonderful, Bobby. Tell me what you're doing with yourself these days."

Robert glanced at the bride something magazines. "Well, Mr. Burris, I'm teaching history at Helton Prep, but I think—"

"No kidding? Good school, Helton. Hell of a school."

"Um, sure is. But I think—"

"Teaching at Helton, eh? You know, Bobby, when you were a student at DeBerry, we were always afraid we might lose you to Helton. When you were a sophomore, I think it was, we were all nervous that Helton might try to steal you with one of those famous Helton basketball scholarships." The old man chuckled raspily. "Your dad sure would've liked that, wouldn't he?"

Robert was sure that Mr. Burris was senile. Robert hadn't been near as good a player as Dad wanted him to be, as far as he could remember. Dad had always said he had no left hand. *That's why you won't play in college. Real players have a left hand. Shooters like you? A dime a dozen.*

"I suppose he would've, yes. He died six years ago." As soon as the words escaped his mouth, Robert was aware that he would never say something so abrupt to his students — and certainly not to her.

Mr. Burris's smile disappeared. "Oh, I'm so sorry, Bobby. So sorry, son."

Robert thought that the silence that followed was awkward, so he told his old teacher about her.

"I'm, ah, I'm getting married in a few months. Love to have you come, Mr. Burris."

The smile came home. "Well, that's wonderful news, Bobby! Who's the lucky girl?"

"She works at First National."

Mr. Burris stood as if waiting for something else. Instead of her name, Robert offered a sheepish grin. Mr. Burris cleared his throat.

"First National. That right? Well, that's terrific, Bobby. I'm happy for you. I'll expect my invitation. Wouldn't miss it for the world."

The silence mounted again. Robert couldn't think of something to say. He was relieved when Mr. Burris opened his mouth to speak. Robert decided to answer one more question politely, and then go ahead and get his hair wet so he could change his sweater in time for Jay and Linda.

"Bet you're coaching at Helton, eh? I don't get to the games much anymore, but I'll bet you love the heat. Nothing like high school basketball, eh?"

"No, sir. I mean, yes, it's great, and I did it for awhile, but I gave it up last year. No time." Robert spread his hands in a 'what-can-you-do?' gesture. "Unfortunately," he added with what he hoped was a rueful grin.

He almost laughed aloud, imagining her sitting in the stands at eight o'clock at night. Two years ago, the night she actually came to his sectional playoff game against Southeast Atlanta, he had looked up from his squat in the coach's box during the second quarter and seen her check her watch. Fourth row, midcourt. He never knew why, in the middle of a fast break by his boys, he looked up at her. And he never quite understood why her checking her watch had seemed to happen in slow motion.

They'd been dating for seven pretty-good months, and he'd thought that if she could just see one of his games, just one, she might catch the fever. What a beautiful, intense, passionate sport. And she was a beautiful, intense, passionate woman. She couldn't help but love it. Who could resist it, if they gave it a real chance? She might even forget what she'd said about his salary being smaller than that midget on "Fantasy Island". But halfway through the third quarter, the trainer passed him a note written on a First National memo sheet. She had some errands to run, and would meet him at Tino's Restaurant at ten-thirty.

They had eventually won by two, on a three-point buzzer-beater by Scott Perry, the reluctant junior Robert had tutored endlessly for three years. The kid *did* it. He really, finally did it. He was sure she would have been moved. After the game, Robert and Scott were mobbed by reporters on the way to joining the jubilant lockerroom celebration.

At Tino's, she replied that that was nice, and then ordered the seafood lasagna to go with her Merlot.

Two months later, over spinach salad with sliced peaches on the side, she offered her opinion that it would be nice if he would grow up a little bit and show some ambition. Perhaps he could quit that coaching silliness.

"Bobby?"

Robert was jolted from his reverie. For a moment, he thought he was back at DeBerry, caught not paying attention to his teacher.

Mr. Burris had a puzzled look on his wrinkled face. Robert was uncomfortably certain that the old man was going to say something preachy about the coaching, just like the headmaster had done nearly two years ago. Something about the importance of impact and following our natural direction. But Mr. Burris just studied Robert's eyes for a few seconds.

"I'm terribly sorry to hear that, Bobby. Sure am."

Robert could not have this conversation. Not now.

He re-focused on the task at hand. She'd be mighty irked if she knew he was wasting time talking to Mr. Burris when he still didn't know which bride something she wanted. He was tempted to tell Mr. Burris about the job he'd accepted at the stock brokerage, but he hadn't told the headmaster about it yet, and Robert believed strongly in courtesy. She wanted him to tell the headmaster right away, to commit himself, but it was only January and contract time was in April. So he'd kept it quiet so that the kids wouldn't find out and be so upset, like they were when he dropped basketball last year. In fact, Scott Perry didn't speak to him for weeks after the announcement. But that was okay, Robert thought now. After all, Scott was at Princeton, living his dream of playing college basketball.

No, he wouldn't tell Mr. Burris about the stock brokerage. Not right this minute. Besides, she would be the first to point out that Mr. Burris probably didn't have any stocks anyway, just like Robert. As a matter of fact, just this morning she had said that if Robert had some of the stocks that Jay had, maybe he could feel better about only being a teacher.

Mr. Burris wouldn't want to hear about that. And that phone call wasn't going to happen by itself. Enough of this awkwardness. Time to get going.

"Well, Mr. Burris, it's— it's great seeing you. I have to finish a couple of errands here. You know. I'll be in the proverbial doghouse if I don't."

Robert tried to cap the remark with a casual laugh, but it emerged as an absurd croak.

Mr. Burris gripped Robert by the wrist and wished him well, and hurried off down the aisle. Robert felt disconcerted by the departing look on Mr. Burris's face. The poor man seemed sad. School was probably all the old man had, sort of like a twenty-first-century Mr. Chips.

As Robert passed the red-haired girl and opened the shop's front door to brave the rain and discover the something he needed to know, a wave of compassion washed over him. If it was okay with her, he would invite Mr. Burris for dinner one night. They could talk about school, and kids, and how some things never change, and enjoy some Bass ales together. Maybe on a Wednesday night or something.

Then maybe Mr. Burris could stick around and talk some basketball. Anything to ease the sadness old people must feel, just waiting without a purpose anymore, their dreams limping behind them like old dogs.

FRIDAY AFTERNOON

T he rusty rear bumper of the sky-blue pickup bore no distractions for Bryce Stanford. Yet, he didn't dare take his eyes off the obnoxious bumper sticker and its contention about Jesus. If the moron in the truck was going to go fifty in a fifty-five, Bryce would just have to let him know that some people on the planet actually had somewhere to be, rednecks notwithstanding. To stay tight in the pickup's rearview, Bryce had to concentrate on Jesus Saves.

Just his luck, too. Late Friday afternoon, stuck in a two-lane nightmare behind Jed frigging Clampett, when the party was starting at seven. Seven! He'd never make it. Not at this rate. What was worse was that Joan's dad was going to ride him anyway, what with those yokels at Burton's dropping the account without even looking at the goddamned numbers. It wasn't as if Marvin needed more fodder for needling his son-in-law.

"Jesus saves **WHAT**, you **MORON?**" Bryce yelled into the windshield, pumping his fist.

As if in answer, the pickup's speed dropped to forty-eight. Bryce imagined the guy in the truck, nothing to do, nowhere to be, such a goddamned redneck, enjoying a chuckle holding up the Bryce Stanfords of the world. Redneck's revenge? A slow pickup on a Friday afternoon.

The northbound traffic was maddeningly heavy. Bryce couldn't find a decent shot at getting around Goober, so he groped for the black flair pen lying on the BMW's tan leather passenger seat. He'd write the loser's license number on his *hand* if he had to. Find out where the gomer worked and get his ass fired, if it was the last thing—

A chance to pass. Not much of a chance, a distant part of him warned, but he was sure the chicken truck coming down the northbound hill was slugging along about as slowly as Goober, who had *no* right, none whatsoever, to make the CEO of a Charlotte company late for *anything*, much less his father-in-law's birthday party. He'd get around him because he deserved to. Besides, he was sick and goddamned tired of Jesus Saves nothing.

Bryce swung the black BMW across the double-yellow and gunned the accelerator, pulling even with the pickup.

Immediately, in a flash of horror, he saw his mistake.

The northbound chicken truck was roaring down the hill, hurtling toward the BMW. Bryce's stomach fell through the seat. Son of a *bitch*, he thought, panic screaming to get back into his lane.

He had time to hit the brakes hard and swing back behind the pickup, but he imagined the goober laughing at him in his rearview, and Marvin's stale wisecracks about the tardy son-in-law who couldn't keep a crow operating in the black. *Nobody understands.*

He pressed the gas all the way to the floor. For an impossible moment, he thought he might just make it. Too late, Bryce recoiled at the mushrooming enormity of the truck's grill, its horn blasting obscenely as he realized that he would have to do something *now*. Right now right now right *now*. He swung the BMW back to the right, cringing, squeezing his eyes shut, closing his mind to the pain that would come as he hit the pickup and careened into the path of the chicken truck.

But the pain never came. Only a flash of white light against the screen of his eyelids as the chicken truck, horn complaining,

Friday Afternoon

rumbled past and Bryce heard the squeal of braking tires behind him. He opened his eyes to steady the BMW, shaking his head to clear the light and see what he needed to see. Heart pounding, he peeked at the rearview mirror in time to see the pickup roll over on its side, its rear half on the shoulder embankment, its front half jutting onto the road. A VW bug swerved to avoid the pickup, but Bryce could not concentrate on that right now.

He wiped his forehead with the back of his right hand, though he wasn't perspiring. *Jesus Christ, that was too goddamned close.* Glancing again into the rearview mirror, he saw the receding sky-blue splotch and shook his head. Catching his breath in deep sucks, he pondered turning around. *The man might have his own party to get to. Or a broken neck. Turn around.*

But the goober was all right, he knew. Just flipped on his side was all. On an embankment at that. Probably could rock it back upright. Hell, it was an old truck, Goober's own fault for slugging along like he was. Highway 16 was traveled by Charlotte professionals all day, men and women of consequence who had to do business in these nuisance small towns. Successful people who helped Goober and his neighbors, anteing up taxes for the hellish roads Goober liked to clog.

But soon Goober and his fellow wastes of oxygen wouldn't have Bryce Stanford to frustrate anymore. Soon, the financing would come through for the internet company he and Steve Warner planned to start. If it didn't come from Marvin it would come from that venture capital firm Steve was in bed with. And that would be the end, the end of these nightmare drives to Mayberry and Hooterville and the rest of these rural yesterday freakshows. *Jesus, that last hellhole didn't even have a McDonald's. Just a "Pit Stop Barbecue". The place looked more like a damned tepee than a restaurant.*

As Bryce settled the BMW in at around seventy (traffic ahead of the pickup had long since disappeared ahead of them), he

15

thought of his last meal. Breakfast had been quick. Just Joan's godawful attempt at poached eggs. But there'd be food at Marvin's birthday party. Would there ever! And—

The sudden rattling staccato of the helicopter was close. Very, very close, enough to make the car shake. Bryce struggled with the wheel as he strained to see where the damned chopper was, and then he remembered Elaine Giddings's flat tire on the way to the sales meeting in Wilmington last year. They had all at first thought a helicopter was hovering overhead, until Elaine had to fight the wheel for control as the flat forced her to pull over.

Oh, good Christ. Not me. Not today. But it was him, and it was today. Bryce rattled the car onto the slender gravel shoulder, careful to stay a few feet from the weedy ditch on the right. Lucky for Goober he didn't flip on *this* stretch, Bryce thought. Nasty truck would've been five feet down in these weeds.

He turned off the ignition and just sat for a few moments, wondering what he had ever done to deserve the life he'd been handed. Running his father-in-law's company, married to a spoiled bitch, having to do half the sales trips himself because Marvin was too cheap to let him hire some help for Bob Schimmel. And now he would be late for Marvin's birthday party, and he would never hear the end of it. Never. *Jesus Saves what, you goober. Not Bryce Stanford. Not Friday afternoon when my goddamned life depends on it.*

Bryce took a deep breath and unhooked the cell phone from its holder between the front seats. He pulled the motor club card from his wallet and dialed the 800 number. An eighteen-wheeler rumbled past, rocking the BMW as Bryce pondered the necessity for the jackass to pass so close to the goddamned shoulder.

As he waited for the connection, he considered whether there were roaming charges for 800 numbers out of his local calling zone. Probably. *Frigging* probably, at least today.

The call didn't connect. The digital phone indicated it was redialing, but Bryce knew the phone too well. That foothill over there, so goddamned picturesque, probably interrupting Bryce's call.

He got out of the car and walked around to the right rear tire. "Jesus Saves donkey dip," Bryce muttered, and opened the trunk.

Bryce stared at the spare, encased in black leather. He'd never changed a flat before, and had no desire to learn now. He turned and peered toward the sinking sun, scanning up and down for any sign that he was close enough to an exit or cross street to walk to a service station.

Of course he wasn't, he mused. He was in the god-forsaken woods. If Jesus Saved, the cell call would go through, or there'd be a big bright Exxon sign decorating the dying afternoon sky.

Another eighteen-wheeler trundled past, followed by a grey Mercedes. *Nice if the guy in the Benz would get past that foothill and call the troopers. Hell, man, it's a Beemer on the shoulder, not some chicken farmer in a pickup.* That distant part of him awakened again to ask a vague echoey question about the shoe and the other foot, but Bryce had real problems to deal with. Darkness was riding fast and tall over the November horizon.

As cars and trucks continued to roar past the wounded BMW as if it wasn't there, anxiety gave way to despair. He would have to try to fix the flat himself. Either that or walk, but walk where? There was no life here, at least not reasonable, civilized. The motor club would send him civilization, but— Hey, that was it. He wouldn't walk to find *someone.* He'd walk to find a place from which to call. Maybe even up the foothill a ways.

He opened the passenger front door and removed the phone. Worth a try, he thought. Just walk up that—

His rising hope was interrupted by the steady sound of crunching gravel approaching from behind the BMW. He turned to face the growing sound, suddenly confident that a trooper's cruiser was rolling up the shoulder to prove that Jesus indeed Saves after all.

Hope gave way to shock as Bryce stared into the approaching muddy grill of the sky-blue pickup, forty yards away and closing. *Jesus, oh **Jesus**. This can't be **real**. No goddamned way. It happened five minutes ago. How can it be the same truck?*

An image flashed. Scavengers enjoying the unhurried luxury of a dark Friday night to ravage Bryce's ripped body behind the cover of the ditch's standing dead weeds. Tattered remnants of his navy pinstripe suit, cast aside to make way for the group gluttony.

The pickup stopped ten yards behind the BMW. Bryce briefly considered running, anything to avoid a confrontation with this man just minutes before dark. But reason won out. What could the guy do, really? The law was on Bryce's side.

Insurance. That was the answer. He'd give the guy his insurance information. Tell him he had planned to turn around and come back, but as the guy could see, he blew a flat before he could return to help. Mighty glad the guy was able to get the pickup upright. Big relief the guy was okay and all that. Here's the insurance. I've got the card.

The driver's door opened. Bryce's stomach tensed as a big paunching man in a checked flannel shirt, rolled up at the sleeves to reveal beefy Popeye forearms, stepped down onto the shoulder's gravel. His hair was disheveled, salt-and-pepper, grown long on top and blowing lightly over a balding pate.

The man slammed the truck's door, giving Bryce a quick view of crisp new blue jeans that surprised Bryce in a Sears thirty-percent-off kind of way. The shirt was old, checked in green and red. The cowboy boots were caked with the same orange-clay mud that crusted the truck's grill. But the jeans were spotless, brand new, stiff like dark blue cardboard.

First the man stood and regarded Bryce from beside the truck. A ruddy, clean-shaven face housed a largish nose, closed thick lips and intelligent eyes which, like the blue jeans, seemed to have been placed on the man by a confused Norman Rockwell. The eyes were a relief. They suggested reasonableness. Respect maybe. Yes, he would just apologize and pull out his insurance ca—

"Got troubles?"

The voice was deep, the "trou" drawn out slowly as if reaching forward to grope for the last syllable in the approaching dusk.

As the man ambled casually toward the BMW, Bryce couldn't help but get the feeling that the man didn't recognize the car. *Impossible*, sense countered quickly. *You don't forget a car that runs you off the road.* But the man's demeanor, hands now thrust into stiff blue pockets, suggested the leisure of someone close to home, unruffled by the impediments of Friday afternoon; nothing close to the frustration or anger of one who has just rocked his pickup upright from a leaning embankment. *The goober doesn't know the BMW. La-la land.*

Now close, the man was taller than he'd seemed from ten yards. About six-three to Bryce's six even.

"Man, do I ever," Bryce replied. He held up the mobile phone. "Can't get through to triple A." Bryce would just match the casualness. *Didn't run him off the road. Didn't run him off the road. Not if he didn't see the car's make or something.*

The distant inner voice returned with a quiet, meek reminder that he had tailgated the gomer for at least ten minutes. Something about BMW's having distinctive fronts, blah blah blah.

"Got a jack in yer car there, pardner? I kin have ya movin' in no time." The man clapped a powerful ham-hand on Bryce's right shoulder.

The man didn't know the car. *Jesus Christ.* Bryce almost burst into laughter. *Jesus Saves. Yes sirree. Gives redneck morons amnesia, or a raging absence of observative skills. Like they say, pal, that's why you're driving that disgusting mudbucket and I'm not.*

Polite. Stay polite. You own this goober. Six ways to Sunday.

"Sure do. Jack's in the trunk here. Thanks a million. How fast can you work? I've got to be in Charlotte by seven."

The big man stepped over to peer down into the trunk.

"Charlotte, huh? Nice city, Charlotte. They got them a mighty fine flea market every first weekend of the month. Gotta like them Panthers, too, sure do." He rummaged in the trunk and withdrew the jack and tire iron, placing them carefully on the gravel before reaching back in with both hands to remove the spare.

"How long ya had this car? Mighty nice vee-hicle."

The man stood waiting for the answer, hugging the spare in his Popeye arms.

"About six months. Thanks. I like it."

"Hell, yes, pardner. What's not to like, ya know?" The man carried the spare around to the flat and set it down like rare china. "Whaddya do, to drive a car like that?"

The big man regarded Bryce with those intelligent eyes, and put his hands back in his pockets.

Bryce shifted uneasily, toeing the gravel with a black wing-tip. "I'm the chief executive officer of a floor-covering whole-saler. Look, I'd love to talk about our employment and all, but I've really got to be in Charlotte by seven. How about I give you twenty dollars to hurry?"

The man's eyes darkened. "Why, I don't want yer money, pardner. You needed help. What kinda citizen would I be if I just let ya sit here stuck, night comin' and all. Some folks around here'd let ya sit here and rot all night. But that ain't right though. Just ain't right. You don't deserve that kinda treatment, just 'cause yer from Charlotte. No, sir. We're gonna get you where yer goin'. No money necessary no how." He began to remove the leather from the spare. "You'd do me the same, I'm sure."

"Oh, absolutely." *Dumb goober.* "Thanks for understanding about the need for speed, mister... what's your name by the way?"

The man removed his massive right hand from the leather and extended it. Bryce accepted the hand and was immediately knee-buckled by the crushing grip. When they let go of the handshake, Bryce could feel the throb of his pulse in his palm and fingers.

"Wilson," came the deep voice. "Wilson Emblen. And you, pardner?"

There was something vaguely distasteful about the man's use of the nickname. Pardner. It reminded Bryce of a carpet buyer in Wilmington who liked to call him "Chief". Bryce had long thought that if the company hadn't needed the buyer's business, he'd have told the buyer where he could stick that insincere "Chief" shit.

"Bryce Stanford. Good to meet you, Wilson. You're a godsend."

"Oh, nothin' worth mentionin'. Like I said, nothin' you wouldn't do fer me."

The man called Wilson threw the tire's leather jacket into the trunk. He picked up the jack and knelt to position it under the BMW's right rear frame. Satisfied, he began cranking the car up.

"Floor coverins, huh?" Wilson called over the rhythmic metallic creaking.

"Um. Yes."

"You like that?"

"Of course. I run the company." What a stupid question. No wonder he didn't recognize the car.

"I know you run the company, pardner." Bryce thought he heard just the slightest twinge of irritation in the man's voice, but it was likely just the rise and fall of the western North Carolina dialect.

"What I mean is, you *like* floor coverins? They mean some-thin' to ya?"

Just fix the goddamned tire.

"Sure, of course. It's my business."

"Yeah, well. Somebody's got to do it, right, pardner?" Wilson laughed as if in appreciation of his own good humor, finished jacking up the car, and turned to face Bryce. "Me, I don't think I could spend one day in your business." He leaned casually against the BMW, and Bryce was suddenly sure that the man's considerable weight would topple the BMW off the jack.

"Careful, Wilson."

"No cause for fret, Bryce is it? Yeah, that ol' Bavarian Motor Works puts them a mighty fine jack in these here cars. So any-ways, I guess somebody's got to sell people floor coverins so's they don't have to walk around on plywood and cement and stuff. Right, pardner?" Wilson looked as if he had all night.

"Well, you make it sound kind of pedestrian, Wilson. It's not."

"Pedestrian? That don't sound good. Sorry about that. Guess there's money in floor coverins anyhow. That's the big thing, ain't it, pardner. That and gettin' where yer goin'."

The big man's eyes made contact with Bryce's.

"Look, I'd, I'd really like to pay you for your time here. Could, could you move a little faster? I really don't have much time."

Wilson heaved himself from the car. "Hell, look at me, lazyin' on ya. I'm sorry about that. Sometimes I lose track of urgency, my wife likes to say. Says so a lot, too, pardner. Okay, where's yer cap key?"

"My what?"

"Yer hubcaps. Nice vee-hicle like this, need a key to take the caps off."

"Oh. I think I saw a velcro pouch in the trunk. Yes, there it is." Bryce retrieved the pouch and handed it to Wilson Emblen.

As he did so, he thought he noticed a smile at the corners of the big man's thick lips, so he forced one of his own.

Emblen ripped open the pouch. "Thanks, chief. Have this turkey off for ya in a second." He popped the hubcap off in an expert ten seconds, then knelt, picked up the tire iron and began loosening the lug nuts.

"Didn't mean to make ya feel bad about yer business, there, pardner. Man's gotta have pride in his work, no matter what he does for a livin'." He placed the first nut on the ground. "Hell, I got floor coverins in my house, just like everybody else. Weren't fer you, I might be gettin' my feet cold."

"Cold? Oh, you mean on concrete instead of carpet."

"That's what I mean. Bright guy, you are, pardner."

As the second nut landed on the gravel beside the spare, Bryce searched for a reason not to think that the big redneck had just spoken sarcastically. Not finding one, he dismissed the observation, just as he had last week when Jane Calley, Bob Schimmel's secretary, had made a comment about how fortunate the company was to have the CEO out on sales presentations just like Bob, at Bryce's salary and all. Something about mixing it up with the little people. He hadn't liked it, not one bit, but dismissed the comment as irrelevant gibberish. Nonsense from a frustrated bitch who hadn't married well.

He decided to humor Wilson Emblen, as it was getting late. And dark.

"Speaking of business, Mr. Emblen. What line of work are you in?"

The third nut bounced heavily off of a round stone.

"You mean today?"

"Of course."

Emblen frowned slightly, as if giving the question some thought.

"I'm in the used-car business."

"Oh. Wow. That's great. That's great. What did you used to do? Sounds like you used to do something else."

Wilson made a grunting sound as he strained to loosen the fourth nut.

"When?"

Good God, what an idiot.

"Before the used car business."

"Oh, nothin' much of interest to a floor coverins magnate like yerself."

Bryce waited for a truck to pass. Then darkening silence again.

"Like you said, Mr. Emblen, a man's got to have pride in his work. So tell me."

"Well, I kinda like to help people get where they're goin'."

Right, Bryce thought. *By going forty-eight in a fifty-five.*

"Were you a mechanic? Or a travel agent?" Bryce laughed aloud, sure that the big man would share a chuckle about the mental picture of this big oaf in cardboard jeans sitting in front of an outdated PC, hooking folks up with the Hawaiian Hilton and a TWA Getaway.

Wilson didn't laugh. He let out a sigh as he stood and stretched his back.

"Shoot, pardner, I need to lose some weight. Back's killin' me. No, sir, not a travel agent."

"What, then?"

"Well, sir, sometimes, when I help people get where they're goin', we talk a little about Jesus."

Oh, God. Here it comes. That's why the crack about money. Why was it, Bryce wondered while maintaining a straight face, that everybody who didn't have money, like blacks and rednecks, was always excusing failure in life by professing an allegiance to Jesus? The most convenient excuse for failure ever invented by man.

"Really. You talk about Jesus, eh?"

"We talk about Jesus." The big man kicked a stone casually. "Figured you knew that already."

A pang of alarm pinged about Bryce's gut like a pinball.

"You, you figured I what?"

"Knew that already. Hell, pardner, you had plenty of time to read the sticker. Just two words. Educated guy like you. What the hell else were you lookin' at? Wavin' yer arms like you was gonna kick my ass."

The big man resumed his crouch and went to work on the fifth nut.

Bryce's mind was ahead of his mouth. He opened both. Neither cooperated.

The fifth nut thudded next to Bryce's left wingtip.

"Funny how folks got so much courage when they're drivin' in their cars. Wonder why that is."

Bryce stared, eyes slightly out of focus, at the nut next to his shoe.

"So what say, pardner, we go have us some supper. No fret. I'll finish her up for ya, and we can go get some of Burt Frye's real good steaks, for Wanda to grill up for us."

What? "I, I have to get back to Charlotte. But I have, I, I have my insurance card for you right — it's right here. It's—" Bryce fished, hands shaking, in both pockets for the insurance card he thought he'd stuffed in a pocket before— that's right, he'd only *planned* to offer the insurance card.

"My card's in the car. I'll just grab it." *Jesus.* Heart pounding, he took a step toward the driver's side, past the rear license plate—

"Don't want no *insurance*, pardner," called the deep voice, tone louder, commanding, freezing Bryce in midstep.

Bryce turned.

"Look, I swear I was going to turn around and come back, but,

but I blew the flat, and I'm glad you're okay, really glad you're okay and, and I was going to say something about it. Really I was. We just got to talking so fast. What...what do you want? I'd like to give you the card, if we could just settle this so I can get—"

"I want to get ya where yer goin'." Wilson Emblen rose again to his full height, hefting the sixth lug nut in his right hand, the tire iron in his left. "Like I said."

"And I, I appreciate that, certainly. Certainly I do. Maybe I could arrange for something to be done for your, for your floors. Hardwood, maybe. My pleasure."

"You believe in God, pardner?"

"Ex—excuse me?"

Wilson Emblen flipped the nut into the air and caught it.

"When you was carryin' on like that in my rearview mirror, how the hell'd ya know whose back you was climbin' up? How'd ya know I wouldn't follow ya to Charlotte, shoot ya in the head? Supper time, comin' up here soon. We'll talk us a little bit about Jesus. Then we'll get ya where yer goin'."

Wilson examined the lug nut as if it were alive.

"Hell, maybe He'll join us. We'll get us some ribeyes just in case. Some red wine. Yeah." Wilson Emblen returned to his work, grunting again as he lowered his bulk to the task. "I'll try to get this done for ya before I can't see. Don't got no flashlight in the truck. You?"

Used car business. Right. Sure.

"Um. No. Listen, I really am sorry. Couldn't we just settle this? You know, financially?"

He's not looking. Wave down this car. This one right here. Might be the last one for a few minutes. He's got plans. Supper my ass. Pop in the head with the tire iron, more likely. Bedtime in the weeds. Wave it down — aw, son of a bitch.

Wilson replaced the old tire with the spare, and began applying and tightening the nuts, one by one.

"Ever think about dyin', pardner? I don't just mean now, or when yer sittin' next to somebody's bed sayin' goodbye." A nut whined as he used his powerful right arm to give an extra quarter turn with the iron. "I'm talkin' about the realization that a whole planetload of boys just like you are dead in the ground. Centuries of 'em. And nobody knows who they were. Fer instance, take when you was takin' social studies class in grade school. Learnin' about the explorers, and generals, and conquistadors, and philosophers, and folks who discovered gravity and math formulas and the planet's shape and wrote them epic poems. Stuff like that. Folks that made a difference. Remembered by someone besides their own families.

"And once in a while they'd explain that there was also merchants. Ya notice that they never had a name for no merchant? Never heard no one, in social studies and history and so on, say 'Hey, now I want ya to learn about the feller who was the richest feller in his town. One hell of a nobleman, or gentry', or some such that they used to say? Nope. Seems the merchants and noblemen and gentry fellers was always just lumped together in social studies class. I always felt sorry for them merchants and gentries when I was a kid. They didn't accomplish nothin'. Before they died. Just sellin' and eatin' and cheatin', just like you. Must've felt like hog manure when they died."

Bryce calculated that he could be behind the driver's seat in three seconds. But how fast could he get the door closed? And locked?

Wilson Emblen tightened the last nut and rose.

"What I want is, I want to get ya where yer goin'. Without the hog manure. Not like them nameless merchants in social studies class. So we can just have some supper and talk about it. You avoidin' becomin' a nameless merchant and all." He picked up the hubcap and dropped it clattering into the trunk. "Then we can get ya where yer goin', especially if Jesus shows up for some ribeye and red."

Insane. Dead bodies under his house.

He couldn't be in the car fast enough, nor could he possibly overpower this man who could snap his neck with one arm. Running was still an option, but Bryce didn't know where he was, and couldn't abide the thought of abandoning the car.

The cell phone. It was still in his pocket. But how would he call? And whom?

"That, that sounds good, Wilson. Ribeye would be nice."

Wilson smiled through the dusky remnants of light. He twirled the tire iron like it was made of plastic.

"Ya mean that?"

"Sure."

"Thought ya had somewheres to be."

"I do, but a ribeye sounds like the ticket." *Grocery store. Help all over the place. Just pretend you give a rat's derriere about this name-less-merchants-and-Jesus nonsense. Hell, he fixed the flat. Trusting moron, but dangerous and insane. Just play along to the grocery store, and home free. Might even get the D.A. going on a kidnapping charge.*

"The ticket. I like that, pardner. Here's yer ticket."

Wilson Emblen hit Bryce Stanford across the left temple with the tire iron, and helped him fall into the trunk with the hubcap.

***

"There, his eyes is openin'. Wanda, say hello to Mr. Bryce Stanford. Two-one-one Chesterton Place. Charlotte."

Cobwebs gave quick way to clarity as the pounding throb of pain beat at the left side of Bryce's head.

The room was small, wallpapered in a yellowed colonial sea-side scene. Bryce found himself seated at a dining table, an old Queen Anne which smelled of lemony Endust. At the other end of the six-seat table sat Wilson Emblen, now clad surprisingly in a fresh blue blazer worn over a white button-down shirt, collar open to reveal a too-tight T-shirt stretched to fit around the base of his thick neck.

Behind Wilson Emblen stood a slight woman with a short sparse patch of white hair, decorated by an unnecessary red barrette worn on the left side of her head, above the temple. Her face was weathered, wrinkled, but her sharp green eyes suggested that while her skin said she was seventy, she might just be fifty. The bright red lipstick, worn against the backdrop of her otherwise unfixed face, looked like it had been applied in the last five minutes.

When she spoke, her voice bore the husky rasp of a lifetime of cigarettes.

"A pleasure to make your acquaintance, Mr. Stanford." The accent was Southern, but not western North Carolina. Genteel, soft. Bryce couldn't quite place it. Georgia, perhaps. Or Charleston.

Without looking under the table, Bryce could feel the pressure, not too tight, of some kind of cloth binding his ankles together. The smell of burnt potatoes drifted from an open pot sitting on a small stack of newspapers in the middle of the table. The combination of lemony Endust and the potatoes was not, given the circumstances, an unpleasant aroma for the room.

"Thank you."

"Pardner, this here's my wife Wanda. Five years my senior, twenty years my wiser, I likes to say."

Bryce tested the strength of the ankle bindings. Some give. Not much. *Don't be obvious.*

"How, how are you, Wanda?"

"Well, I'm just *delighted* you could join us for supper, Mr. Stanford. Very kind of you to change your plans, all on account of Our Lord."

She turned and removed some plates from a well-preserved Queen Anne china cabinet next to an unadorned window. The

window framed pitch darkness and a reflection of the tar-
nished chandelier's light. Wanda set the plates down next to
the potatoes.

"There," she said, as if accomplishing a day's worth of work.

Bryce counted four plates in the stack.

"Pardner," came Wilson's deep voice from across the table.
He slid his seat back on the wooden floor. "I need to know how
ya like yer steak. They'll be past rare by now. Pink or gray?"

Keep the words even. Steady. *He likes to talk.*

"Pink for me. Thanks." *Think of where you are.* "No, make that
well-done, if you would."

"Gray it is. Like it pink myself. Wanda here don't eat red
meat, so I'm grillin' up a nice breast a chicken. Jesus likes it
gray like you, so don't fret about puttin' me out and all." Wilson stopped and regarded Bryce from the cased opening, which
Bryce presumed led to an outside door.

"He'll be here presently," said the big man, and he turned
and clomped down an unseen hall. Bryce heard the sound of
a screen door squeak open, then slam shut three times, the coil
too tight or too loose; Bryce never knew which.

The woman stood staring at the potatoes. She touched the
handle of the serving spoon which stood straight up from the
middle of the bowl, held there by the surrounding weight of
the food. After a few seconds, she began to mechanically stir
the potatoes.

If he could reach her, just get one hand around that chick-
en-wire wrist, he could trade her neck for his own. The thought
made him feel queasy, though. He'd have to be willing, and
able, to break her neck if Wilson called his bluff. Briefly, almost
subconsciously, he wondered whether he would call an intrud-
er's bluff if Joan were in danger.

Wilson had referred repeatedly to getting Bryce where he
was going. On reflection, it seemed that those comments might

be cryptic threats from a man who enjoyed messing with his mind. Such a man might be looking through this window right now, rather than tending the grill, just to see what Bryce would do alone with this tiny woman.

Bryce selected inaction.

"So, Wanda. Who's the other guest? I see you have four plates."

Wanda emerged from her reverie.

"Our Lord Jesus Christ." She began stirring the potatoes, which seemed strange given that they were russets. "My husband just told you. Don't you listen, Mr. Stanford?"

"Well. Yes, I listen, Wanda. But I've never met, um, Jesus Christ, and now you're telling me I'm having dinner with the son of God. In your home. Why would he come here?"

"Because you are a desperate soul, Mr. Stanford. Lucifer plans to take you tonight." She returned to the china cabinet and took out four salad plates. "Now please hush, so that I may prepare the table."

As Emblen's wife arranged the other three place settings, apparently leaving Bryce's setting to Wilson, Bryce furiously reviewed the facts as he remembered them. They were attempting, he was pretty sure, to *convert* him in some screwed up, backwoods way. Either that or they were playing a game, some kind of macabre preface to murder.

He tried to look out the uncovered window, but the darkness outside was so total that all he saw was his reflection. Clearly there were no neighbors, at least none who worried the Emblens as potential whistleblowers.

Bryce strongly preferred the conversion theory. That must be where this wacko guest would come in.

He would be ready. Sales, after all, was his business.

Soon Wilson returned from the grill, the pleasing smell of the ribeyes arriving almost ahead of the clap-clap-clap of the screen door.

Wilson set the platter of steaks down on the stack of newspapers next to the potatoes, and heaved himself wearily into his seat.

"I'll tell ya what, pardner. I need one a them gas grills. What a blamed mess. Damned charcoal. Aw, *hell*, woman, why didn't ya tell me I needed to set his place before I set down?" Emblen grunted as he slid back the chair, rose, and picked up a salad plate, dinner plate and silverware. He retrieved a linen napkin from the china cabinet, and went about setting Bryce's place.

Bryce noted that the big hands set a butter knife next to Bryce's spoon. The other three settings, out of reach, were furnished with steak knives. Bryce reflected that he had underestimated Wilson Emblen several times since first pulling the BMW close to the pickup's rear. He would not do it again.

Wanda Emblen poured four glasses of cabernet into beautiful tall wine glasses. *Everything's nice, considered, so why the stack of newspapers?...Why the cardboard blue jeans worn that afternoon, with the old shirt and boots, the clay-encrusted old truck? Nothing fits quite exactly. So how does this Jesus wacko fit in?*

As if in answer, the doorbell rang. Traditional ding-dong, coming from the direction of the room's other cased opening.

Wilson had just set Bryce's wine glass near the right corner of his red placemat.

"He's a smidge early. Set up straight, pardner."

Bryce adjusted his posture.

Wanda smoothed her flower-patterned dress, touched her barrette lightly, and left the room somberly.

"I, I didn't hear a car pull up, Wilson."

Wilson stood expectantly near the cased opening, and spoke without facing Bryce.

"Pardner, the Nazarene don't need no automobile."

Bryce heard the front door open, followed by some unintelligible greeting from Wanda. Then he heard the strangest thing he'd ever heard in his life:

"Thank you, ma'am".

It wasn't the words that puzzled Bryce. It was the voice. The boy who spoke them couldn't have been older than seven or eight.

Wanda entered the room first, holding the hand of a young boy with blond hair, brush-cut like a young Johnny Unitas. The boy was indeed about seven. He wore a striped, collarless short-sleeved shirt, reminiscent to Bryce of many shirts he had worn as a boy growing up in the early sixties. The shirt was tucked neatly into a pair of faded but clean blue jeans, held up by a thick brown belt with a brass buckle. His shoes looked like old-fashioned Keds that had received plenty of wear. The look on the boy's handsome face was shy, but his eyes found Bryce's immediately, and held them without a hint of emotion.

"Well, looky what the cat drug in," Wilson exclaimed. "Here, have a seat right here."

Wilson offered a long look at Wanda, then pulled out the chair to the right of Wilson's, and hoisted the boy into the seat. The boy's legs didn't reach the floor, so Wilson slid the chair in for him.

"Thank you, sir." The boy's voice was soft, but remarkably clear, and devoid of accent. "Sir, could I have some cheese and crackers?"

"Of course, pardner," Wilson said as he lowered himself into his seat. "Wanda?"

Wanda stood silently for a moment, and left the room through the doorway she had passed through a minute before.

"Mr. Bryce Stanford, I'd like you to meet Pablo. Pablo, this is Mr. Stanford. Mr. Stanford's tryin' to find his way."

Pablo? The boy looked to Bryce like fifth generation Kansas. *Pablo my ass.*

"Nice to meet you, Pablo."

The boy looked at Bryce and said nothing.

Wilson Emblen broke the silence. "Pablo here is in the second grade. Wouldn't that be right, Pablo?"

Bryce thought he recognized a tone of deference in Emblen's voice.

"That would be right, sir." The boy held his gaze on Bryce. When he spoke again, he spoke to Bryce.

"Sir, would you like to know what we learned about in school today?"

Just go along. Pacify, patronize. Sell, sell, sell.

"I sure would. Pablo."

Pablo took his right forefinger and stuck it in his right nostril, then removed it and traced the rim of his wine glass, inspiring slight ripples in the maroon liquid. His eyes focused on Bryce's.

"We learned about the nameless merchants."

Panic's early-to-rise cousin, Misgiving, rattled awake in Bryce's abdomen.

*Be on your game. This is **not happening**.*

"You learned about...hey, that's terrific...that's terrific, Pablo."

"Why is that terrific, sir?" The eyes. They never went away. *Look at your wine, kid. What the hell are you doing drinking wine, anyway? Or the wallpaper. See the boats? Where's Wanda?*

"Why, it's terrific if you're learning something, Pablo. That's what I meant." Bryce took a sip, a long slurpy one, to give his eyes somewhere else to go. He examined a spot on the glass as if it held some point of curiosity.

"We learned about the nameless merchants, sir. We learned about the nameless merchants who watched a man get his wrists nailed to a cross. Teacher said it was the hands, but I know better. So do the nameless merchants. Want to know why, sir?"

Bryce opened his mouth, but just shook his head.

"Because you can't nail a man by the hands. They'd tear right off, sir."

Bryce's mind floundered for some reason, any reason, why this handsome blond boy with the Johnny Unitas brushcut would have a theory about crucifixion. *Some crazy brainwash job? Is Wilson capable of that? This kid doesn't seem to NEED Wilson.*

Bryce knew his life was on the line, and it had something to do with this kid. Something about getting where he was going. *Say something, or he'll look a hole in your eyeballs.*

"You, you know, Pablo, I never knew that. Never knew that. I—"

"We learned about the nameless merchants who watched a man get his head chopped off for not saying a king was head of a church." It was as if the boy hadn't heard him.

"We learned about the nameless merchants who watched a lady get hanged on a real hot day for letting her son bring some friends home. We learned, sir, about the nameless merchants who watched their neighbors ride off in trucks they didn't want to ride in, then bought their neighbors' stuff cheap, from soldiers in gray coats."

Wanda cleared her throat softly from the hallway, and entered with a plate of sliced cheddar cheese and triscuits. She set the plate to the right of Pablo's placemat, and returned quietly to her seat.

Pablo examined the cheese and crackers, and helped himself. "Thank you, ma'am," he said through a full mouth.

Go ahead. He's a kid. Say what you say to a kid. Catch him off guard.

"You know, Pablo. You really shouldn't speak with your mouth full."

The eyes returned. Bryce looked away.

The boy swallowed the food and looked at Wanda Emblen. "Ma'am, these crackers are real good. You were very nice to get them just for me." He smiled a sweet smile, which she did not return. Her hand reached automatically for the potato spoon and began stirring the russets, which Bryce remotely considered were getting cold.

Wilson spoke. "Pardner, Pablo's a guest in the house. I'd

watch your own manners."

"Ex-excuse me, Wilson. But I have to ask you a question." Anything to look away from the boy. "How do you and Pablo know each other? I mean, where are his parents? He comes here for dinner on a Friday night, by himself, in the dark?" *Or do you keep him locked away in the fruit cellar, a kid with a face on a milk carton somewhere? How long was I unconscious, Wilson? Long enough to "educate" this poor kid about the "nameless merchants"? You're scaring the shit out of me with this stupid game.*

But a game it was, and Bryce would play it out. If Wilson and his wife thought the kid was Jesus Christ, let them. And let "Him" eat his cheese and crackers and try to freak him out. They'd hear what they wanted to hear from Bryce Stanford. That was *his* game, and he was the best.

The boy took a bite of a cracker and cheese, and answered before Wilson could speak.

"If I had parents, sir, they'd tell you it's none of your business." The boy eyed the steaks as if seeing them for the first time. "Steaks. Those look good, sir."

Wilson pulled himself out of his chair. "Speakin' of manners, pardners, I need to watch my own. How you like yours, Pablo? I forget sometimes."

"Well, sir, I like it however you like it."

Wilson looked at his wife, then at Bryce.

"Got one right here, nice and done. Miz Emblen and I just need to talk in the kitchen for a couple minutes."

"Okay, sir."

Bryce watched Wilson and his wife pause at the window, peer out momentarily into the darkness, then walk carefully from the room. For the first time, he wanted them to hurry back. And yet he wondered what they were up to.

Pablo put his half-eaten cracker on his salad plate, and turned again to face Bryce.

"I think he's a big fat redneck turd," the boy said, and retrieved his cracker.

"You—you think he's what?"

"You don't think so, sir?"

"Well, Pablo, it isn't that I—"

"He's a big fat redneck turd." Pablo managed to get the rest of the cracker into his mouth. "He put your car in Louie's back yard," he said, the possessive 's' blocked by the mangled triscuit.

Bryce glanced at the doorway, and out the windows into the black nothingness. Then he turned to face the boy.

"Pablo," he whispered. "Do you know how to get to Louie's?" *Please, God.*

"Sure, sir. I play there all the time. Louie's got Nintendo."

The eyes were on Bryce's again, but Bryce saw an opening in them, something like an invitation. *Now or never.*

"Pablo, if you help me find my car, right now, I'll buy you and Louie all the latest Nintendo. And Sega. Can you—can you take me to Louie's?"

Pablo twisted in his chair to look for signs that the Emblens were returning from the kitchen, or wherever they had gone.

"I think so, sir. Why?"

Why? Dumb kid, after all.

"Well, I want my car, Pablo. It's my car. You'll understand when you're older. And I want to go home. I shouldn't be here, Pablo."

"Oh, sir, that's silly. I think you should be here, sir." Another chomp, on another cracker.

Listen, you wiseass little Hitler youth punk—

"Pablo. I don't live here. Neither do you. The Emblens, I think, have us both here against our will...Can you understand that?" *Stop looking at me like that, god damn it.*

"You really are silly, sir. They're nice people, if you haven't noticed. But sir?"

What now, psycho?

"Yes?"

"I know you want to leave here, sir. After all, you're a nameless merchant like the teacher says." Another maddening bite of cheddar and triscuit. "But can—" The little mouth was too full. Pablo swallowed part of the food and continued. "But can you tell me one thing, sir."

It didn't sound like a question.

Just ask me your sick-puppy question so we can get on with it.

"Pablo, I can tell you one thing, if you can take me to my car."

"I can take you to your car, sir. So, sir...Besides leaving here, what's the one thing you want more than anything else in the whole wide world?"

The eyes, fixed on Bryce's, somehow grew more intense, searching.

*Think about this now. This is probably a setup, some kind of test. Wilson and Wanda are listening from the hallway or something. It's **their** question, not this little kid's. All of it's been theirs. He's programmed, that's what it is. Emblen is a genius.*

Make it good.

"Well, Pablo. What I want more than anything else in the world is, is not to be a nameless merchant. You've helped me with that, you and those nice Emblens, and I'm grateful. I want to see my friends at church, the other deacons like me, and tell them that we should try to accomplish something more than the accumulation of money. Tell them that piling up money and, um, and standing by, while injustices were done right in front of them, was what separated the nameless merchants from the real heroes of human history." **Please** *look at your cracker, even just when you take a bite.* "And, and—"

"What's a deacon, sir?"

Someone with the manners not to interrupt an elder, you little—

"Why, Pablo, a deacon is a leader within a church congrega-tion. Deacons meet regularly and talk about how to make the church better, and how some of the church's money should be spent, and sometimes usher on Sundays. It's service to others, Pablo. Something I deeply, deeply believe in."

Pablo smiled.

"That's wonderful, sir. Got any poor deacons at your church?"

"Any— any what?"

"Poor deacons." The smile disappeared, the eyes shifting to the window and back in less than a second.

"Why, why sure we do. We have poor deacons. Even home-less deacons, Pablo. Because we care, Pablo, or we wouldn't be deacons."

"My teacher says the nameless merchants pile up some of their money by being deacons, sir. By being deacons and city council people and stuff like that. Teacher says it's a real good way to keep the money with the nameless merchants, and away from the people who do the real work."

Pablo started in on yet another cheddar cracker, and took a slurp of wine to wash down the first bite. When he returned his gaze to Bryce's eyes, his lips were a glowy maroon in the chandelier's light.

Little punk's just trying to get a rise out of you.

"Pablo, I'm going to tell you something about your teacher, and then maybe we can go find my car, so I can buy a bunch of stuff for you and Louie." Bryce listened for any indication that the Emblens were near. Silence.

"Your teacher is sick, Pablo. You shouldn't be learning about the things your teacher has been telling you. It's giving you bad thoughts. Do you want to grow up with bad thoughts? No, of course not. Your teacher is just wrong, Pablo. There are lots of good deacons and city council people."

"You're being silly again, sir. But I believe you." A sip of wine. "I'll take you to your car."

Bryce looked furtively at the doorway.

"Pablo, you're going to be a good young man some day. I'm proud of you."

Pablo smiled again. "Thank you, sir. I don't want to have bad thoughts. My teacher is very sick, and I'm glad there are poor deacons at your church."

The boy set his glass down and craned his neck to see down part of the hallway the Emblens had entered.

"Sir?" he called toward the hallway. "Ma'am?"

A distant shuffling, and then footsteps on the hall's wood floor. Wilson and his wife appeared.

Wilson coughed. It sounded forced. "Sorry we took so long, pardners. Lookin' fer the A-1. Wanda always misplaces it when we're expectin' company."

"Sir, if it's okay, I'm going to take Mr. Stanford to find his car." Pablo held his arms up, clearly a request to be lifted from the chair.

Mrs. Emblen spoke, while looking at the cold potatoes.

"Is he— Is he *certain* he wants to go? I mean, he hasn't had anything to eat. We could just sit down and have some—"

"Wanda." Wilson's voice was uncharacteristically terse.

Mrs. Emblen took to stirring the russets, as Wilson lifted the boy out of the chair and set him down. The boy immediately clambered under the table and untied Bryce's ankles, and scrambled back out next to Bryce's right side.

When the boy took hold of Bryce's right hand, Bryce was surprised by the boy's tight little grip.

"Get up, sir. I'll take you to your car, since that's what you want."

Bryce pushed his chair back and stood, not quite sure what to make about this turn of events. The boy continued to hold his hand.

Wilson shifted his big frame uneasily. "Guess Pablo will get you where yer goin', pardner. It's been a pleasure. Sure appreciate yer patience."

Bryce considered several witty thank-yous, but said nothing. After all, the man had hit him in the head with a tire iron. The boy pulled him in the direction of the window-side cased opening, and Bryce could now see that what lay beyond it was a well-appointed foyer. They passed Wanda, her head down, still stirring her russets.

Fifteen more feet. Almost there.

And the doorbell rang.

The stirring spoon clanged against the side of the potato bowl, as Wanda smoothed her dress again, touched her barrette with her right hand, and said chirpily, "I'll get it."

She brushed past Pablo and Bryce to the front door. Pablo tightened his grip.

So did Bryce.

Mrs. Emblen opened the door, and gasped.

"Why, Snood McClain! I declare, I was wondering when your handsome face would show itself. You *darling* man."

The voice that came from around the door struck Bryce as absurdly friendly, almost certainly insincere.

"Wanda Emblen, I swear, on a Friday night you're like a rose light in the darkness."

"Oh, go *on*, Mr. McClain. Go *on*. Come in, come *in*. You'll catch your death out there."

The man entered, nodded at Wilson, and turned to face Bryce. He did not look at the boy. The man's face was pock-marked, the permanent results of what must have been a wicked case of teenage acne. He wore an Atlanta Braves baseball cap, dirty with orange clay, a plain white T-shirt with a faded coffee stain at mid-chest. His khaki pants were wrinkled, and bore several streaks of the familiar Carolina clay.

What struck Bryce most about the man, though, was the fact that he wasn't wearing any shoes.

What a goddamned circus.

"Well, now, Wanda, you look to have a fine guest tonight. Mister...?"

"Stanford," replied Bryce, resisting a sudden urge to kick the man where it really hurts. *What miserable damned timing.*

The boy spoke assertively, looking at the newcomer's belt-less khakis.

"We were just leaving, sir." A pull toward the door.

"Oh? Please tell me I'm not late, Wanda?"

"Oh, of course not, sweetheart." *Touch that barrette...there you go.* "Pablo stopped by for some cheese and crackers."

"Yes, sir," said Pablo. "And Mr. Stanford wants to find his car. Don't you, Mr. Stanford?"

Good boy. Nintendo 'til the sky turns green, my fine child.

"Yes, I'm afraid so. Have to be in Charlotte for a party. I'm very late."

The man looked disappointed, as if stood up by an old acquaintance. "I'm sorry. I love to meet new folks. Maybe I can get you where you're going, instead of Pablo, after we fill our bellies with Wanda's indubitably exquisite repast."

So full of shit. Come on, out with it. Or shall we wait until your belly's indubitably full, before you join the psycho parade about the nameless goddamned merchants?

"Appreciate it. Really do. But Pablo's nice enough to take me to my car."

The man looked at the boy for the first time. "Oh? Before dinner?" He looked back at Bryce. "Sure you won't stay for some casual conversation? Wanda, you could put on some of that Stan Getz fellow, that gorgeous album with the sax and the strings," he said without turning to her. "I could listen to that forever."

*And I could watch you drown. Go wash that filthy shirt. And get me **out** of here.*

"Look, I'm sure I could too. Getz is my favorite, but I really must be going." Bryce tried to release Pablo's hand. "Pablo, I'd like to shake Mr. Emblen's hand, thank him for fixing my tire."

And for the pop in the head, I'll swear out that warrant first thing in the morning.

Wilson extended his hand for the second and last time. Bryce was ready, and braced himself, but this time the big man's grip was gentle, the hand dry and warm.

"Pardner, travel safe. Sorry to see ya go so soon, but I know it's important to ya to get where yer goin'. Pablo, you take good care of Mr. Stanford. Mighty dark out there. Mighty damn dark."

"Yes, sir. Won't stop 'til we find his car, sir. Such a nice car, too."

Wanda examined the left shoulder of her dress with minute care, as Pablo took Bryce's hand again and led him out the door and into the dark toward the civilization which lived in the BMW.

As the boy's firm grip pulled him further from the house, Bryce was oddly disturbed by the total blackness of the night. It had been a clear afternoon. Cloud cover must have rolled in right after dusk. Obscured the stars. After all, he was unconscious for God knows how long. But completely black? He couldn't see six inches ahead of him.

To reassure himself, he looked back toward the house, just so he could *see* something. The house was there, more inviting than he wished to think about right this minute. It receded slowly as Pablo led him confidently in the direction of Louie's and a thankful reprieve. Bryce saw the glow of the Emblens' uncovered dining room windows. He could just make out the potato bowl riding high atop the ridiculous stack of newspapers.

He saw Wanda Emblen enter the room, carefully carrying something flat in her arms. Bryce squinted to see what it was. Wanda set the flat object down on the table and picked up the potato bowl with her right hand. With her left, she picked up the object, and it flopped slightly. Bryce could see what it was.

It was a newspaper.

Bryce resisted the boy's strengthening pull, as Wanda Emblen placed the newspaper on top of the yellowed stack. She turned toward the window and, with her right hand, took her left shoulder sleeve and dabbed at her eyes.

And standing alone, in the front doorway, silhouetted by the foyer light, was the man Wanda referred to as Snood McClain. He stood motionless, his ballcap sitting slightly sideways against the light. The door was wide open behind him, an invitation to return.

Ha! Go on in, Mr. McClain. Eat your indubitable repast. I'll put my own Getz on the Bose, my man. At least we have that in common.

As if the man had heard him, the ballcap turned before the man's body did. The bill bent slowly, mournfully downward. And the door closed.

Bryce pointed his attention again into the dark. The boy was pulling mighty hard for such a runt.

They had walked another twenty paces or so when, vaguely bothered by the boy's apparent confidence that they wouldn't bump into a tree in this black blindness, Bryce turned again to gaze at the house.

Black. It wasn't there. Just the immense pitch pressing aggressively against his eyeballs.

He'd wanted to see the house. Needed it. Had a wild hair to race to the door. Embrace the man in the Braves cap. Offer the man his shoes. Listen to Getz and Gilberto. Enjoy a ribeye and red. Chat about flea markets with the Emblens. Just be in no hurry at all.

"Hey. Pablo. How—how far is it to your friend's? I might want to go back to the Emblens' for a while."

"Oh, sir, don't be silly. We have time." The voice came as little more than a whisper, but the darkness was so silent that the last three words rang loud like a church bell.

"I didn't *ask* how much time we have, Pablo. Wise to watch your manners, son. I asked you how far to Louie's."

"Never you mind, sir." Pablo stopped walking. Bryce's eyes still couldn't seem to adjust quite yet, *so damned black*, but he sensed that Pablo turned to look up at him.

"Never you mind, sir. You want to find your car. We have lots and lots of time."

The boy started walking again, the pull growing stronger.

"Be there when we get there, sir. I promise. Oh, sir, and by the way."

"By the way, what?" Bryce asked, growing irritated by his inability to see a single goddamned thing. *Adjust, goddamn it.*

"The man in the chicken truck is alive, sir. Not that you were curious. But Louie tells me he'll never walk again." The whisper was punctuated by a wintry giggle. "The poor fellow will curse your memory, defecate on it, from now to the end of his days. Nice to be remembered."

The man tried in vain to see the boy. "Pablo, saying things to get a rise from someone is a good way to get hurt, son. I, I didn't hit that chicken truck. You—"

"Louie calls that 'delicious memory', sir. Real tasty, he says. The living cursing the dead. They both lose. Real, real tasty. But, sir, I don't want to get a rise out of you. I just thought you might like updates." Again the frigid giggle. "While we look for your car."

A cold pang of panic coursed through the man's abdomen. "Updates? Listen, you little shit, I want you to take me back to the Emblens. I'm tired of your insolent crap."

The boy's giggle graduated to laughter, growing deeper. Older.

"Updates, sir. Lots and lots of updates. Like your wife, sir.

Now she can marry that man, the one who makes her feel so good on Friday afternoons. Now they can feel good whenever they want. Maybe mock your memory by leaving your picture up to watch them. Updates, sir. While we look for your car. And sir?"

"Take me back there *now*." Tears welled in the man's eyes as he tried to swallow the aching ball growing in his throat.

"Sir, I wonder whether you'd think it was insolent crap if I told you I've forgotten your name."

"**NOW**, goddammit, or I'll have to—what did you say?"

"Your name. Forgot it, sir." Again the giggle. "And so have you."

GRATUITY

❄ ❄ ❄

The couple in the second red booth was having an argument. The man, fortyish with slicked-back blond-white hair, was wearing an expensive charcoal overcoat. Even inside the restaurant. The red-haired woman, perhaps his wife and perhaps not, was listening and looking around. Listening and looking around. Shushing him. The man raised his voice. He said they weren't coming back to this restaurant. Not ever. Not ever, dammit. The woman whispered, loud enough for Hubert to hear, that the man was embarrassing her. To please stop it. To stop it for God's sakes. For God's sakes please stop it you're embarrassing me.

The man did not stop it. He said, and Hubert wasn't the only one who heard him, "If they want to advertise great service, then I have the right to advertise that they don't deliver on what they advertise."

Hubert thought it was odd, almost funny, that the man used the word "advertise" three times in one sentence. Maybe he could have used it once, and then could have said "I have the right to complain" and then "that they don't deliver on what they promise." But the man said "advertise" three times. Hubert didn't know whether to tell him or not. Maybe he would tell him. Maybe the woman would tell him. Yes. She could tell him: "For God's sakes, don't say the word three times in one sentence. You're embarrassing me."

But the woman did not tell him that. She just said "You're

im*pos*sible" and then she smiled, and then said she wanted a refill of her iced tea. The man said, and loud at that, "Maybe if we pitch freaking tents and get a good night's sleep, your iced tea will arrive in the morning." The woman laughed and told the man again how impossible he was.

She seemed to like his impossibility, or was it his impossibleness? She held his hand now, and Hubert thought that was strange, almost funny, since the man embarrassed her and was impossible and used the same word three times in one sentence. Hubert didn't know whether to remind her of how embarrassed she was. He considered reminding her that less than a minute ago she was so embarrassed for God's sakes. He could say here's your unsweet tea ma'am and why are you holding the hand of a man who is impossible and says words like advertise three times in one sentence.

Hubert approached the table.

"Would you like a refill of your tea, ma'am?"

The woman looked at the man and did a snort thing, a snorty laugh thing, like Hubert remembered doing in church when he was a kid and his sister whispered something funny and he was caught off guard and laughed through his nose snortily and after the service his dad smacked him in the head a bunch of times when they got to the car. Hubert considered smacking the woman in the head a bunch of times, but someone else was her dad and it wasn't Hubert and it wasn't the man in the overcoat.

The man picked up the woman's glass and rattled it back and forth, the ice cubes clinking the sides. Hubert worried that the man might crack the glass with all the rattling. "This week if you don't mind," said the man. The woman did the snorty thing again, and Hubert reached up and felt at the right side of his head, remembering his dad. When his dad smacked him that day for disrespecting the minister and God's house and God and Jesus and Mary, there was a smack for all five, not just one. You disrespected the *minister* (smack) and God's *house* (smack) and *God* and *Jesus* and *Mary* (yes, Hubert reflected, it had been five smacks). Again Hubert considered smacking the woman, but reminded himself that somewhere she had her own dad and it must be okay with him that she was with this impossible man for God's sakes. Hubert didn't think that her dad taught her the snorty laugh thing, but if he did it was his business and not Hubert's.

Hubert looked at the man and smiled. "Seven days is a long time, sir," said Hubert.

The man's face reddened. "What the hell did you just say to me, boy?"

The man held the glass up toward Hubert and rattled it again.

"I said I think I can get a refill of unsweet tea for the lady in less than a week, sir," Hubert said, accepting the glass from the man. "Probably a lot less. I pride myself on good service, and I'm not impossible. For God's sakes."

The woman gasped and then did the snorty thing again. She brought her open palms to her face.

The man in the charcoal overcoat said "You impertinent piece of…" and then said "I want to see your manager" and then said "You're through."

Hubert turned and walked to the beverage station behind the cash register, stepping around the fake ficus tree and its pose next to the sales counter. The ficus tree always bothered him in its absence of the need for water. He again considered saying so to the manager, but as the manager was not in at the moment, Hubert figured that he would simply replace the woman's unsweet tea this week rather than next, as requested by the impossible man.

There would be plenty of time for her to get another refill this week, but Hubert preferred promptness, and of course there was also plenty of time to pursue a living ficus tree for the restaurant. All in good time, he thought, and he must have his priorities in place. Maximum customer service was paramount. The manager liked to say "paramount." In order to provide maximum customer service and respect the word "paramount," Hubert selected two unwrinkled packets of Splenda to present to her in appropriate anticipation of her needs.

When Hubert arrived with the woman's refill, the man slapped his right palm on the table and said "We'll take the check."

But paramount customer service is what we advertise, Hubert thought. It's what we value. It's a core value, said the lady from the home office in Florida when she came in to train them last month. A core value, she said. There are five.

"Doesn't the lady want her refill of tea?" Hubert asked, extending the glass toward the woman.

"She wanted it yesterday, friend," said the man in the overcoat. "Now bring the check, please. See, Rhonda, I can be polite, even to people who steal my money with slow service and undercooked sirloins."

Hubert tried to remember whether he knew the man. It didn't seem that they were friends, but he reviewed his friends in his brain for a second or two, and came to the conclusion that whatever was causing the man to say "advertise" three times in a sentence was also plaguing the man's memory. And he had not seen the woman yesterday in the restaurant, or surely he would have provided her with a refill of unsweet tea then. Customer service was as paramount yesterday as today. That was the core value the Florida lady called Consistency. Maybe she sat in Margo's section yesterday. Yes, he thought. That must have been it. Maybe at one of the tables by the mirrors and the fake palm tree that didn't need water one bit more than the ficus did.

"I'm sorry that she didn't get it, sir."

The man stared at Hubert. "Get what?" He seemed annoyed.

"Her refill yesterday. I'll look into it for you."

Again the man's face grew dark.

"Listen, you wiseass. You mock me and I'll cut off your family jewels."

Hubert thought it was odd that the man would offer such a deal, but it didn't seem fair, or even realistic, that the man would know where to find Hubert's family's jewels. His mother died four years ago.

"My mother died four years ago, sir. They were hers. I'm not mocking you, sir. I'm just trying to give you paramount service."

Hubert felt a little bit sick talking to the impossible man, especially when the woman snorted again as the man held his hands out wide and opened his mouth and shook his head. Hubert left to prepare the check. While he did so, he searched for a reason why the man would want to cut off Hubert's family's jewels. He didn't think there were many family jewels, but the main point was that the man was rude to say so. Rudeness and redundancy seemed to be the man's problems, so in that moment Hubert decided to help him.

Hubert brought the check to the table. The man wordlessly threw a Visa card onto the table, and Hubert just as wordlessly picked it up and went back to the cashier station to ring up the bill. He looked at the card. Richard W. Coxhead, it said. Richard W. Coxhead liked to say "advertise" three times in one sentence. Richard W. Coxhead thought that Hubert was an impertinent piece of something. Richard W. Coxhead dramatically, even wildly, overestimated how long it takes to prepare an unsweet tea. Versatile articulation, common sense and measurement were not Richard W. Coxhead's strengths, Hubert decided. Richard W. Coxhead was also impossible and embarrassed his wife or not his wife, but could make her snort with the best of them. That was one of Richard W. Coxhead's strengths. Not among his strengths was the fact that Richard W. Coxhead gave strange instructions like telling people to mock him, the deal being that he would cut off people's family jewels in return. An odd man was Richard W. Coxhead.

Yes, Hubert thought. He could help this man. He could help Richard W. Coxhead. Or was it Rick? Rich? Dick?

R.W.?

Hubert brought back the check and the man's credit card.

Hubert bowed. "It's been a pleasure to serve you, sir. Ma'am."

Richard W. Coxhead laughed, and the woman snorted.

Hubert was confused. He turned and walked back to the cashier station, his heart pounding. This had happened before, this sense of responsibility for others. Their laughter in response to his paramount customer service, especially when he dutifully delivered the lie about pleasure, a lie which the lady from Florida said was a virtue of paramount customer service, made him get that hot feeling again in his stomach. He owed them something, and yet he wasn't sure this time what it was.

The couple got up from the second red booth. The man buttoned his overcoat, and it occurred to Hubert that, oh yes, that was it, wearing the overcoat during lunch saved him from having to put it on as part of leaving. Smart, Hubert thought, to save a step. Hubert reflected that he had underestimated the man based strictly on his weaknesses in vocabulary and common sense and measurement, and that the man's ability to plan ahead was evidenced by the saved step of not having to put on his overcoat to go outside. The woman, on the other hand, had to make three attempts to swing her left arm into and through the left sleeve of the fur-trimmed black leather knee-length coat which she had folded next to her in the booth while eating. Remotely, Hubert considered that the man should have helped his wife or not his wife with the coat, and Hubert concluded that the woman must be his wife after all. If she was not his wife, and they were holding hands during lunch, then he would have helped her with her coat. Hubert was pretty sure of that.

The front door's bell tinkled when the couple stepped out into the cold afternoon air, and tinkled again when the door closed. Hubert went directly to the second red booth and picked up the signed credit-card receipt left behind by the man. The receipt was on top of the vinyl folder, the ball point pen spreading the paper open as if to make sure it could easily be read. The amount with tax said $23.56. On the tip line, written in the blue ballpoint's ink, was a word, rather than numbers and decimals. The word was written in block letters. It said **NADA**.

Hubert stood staring down at the word. **NADA**. He looked over at the closed front door. He looked back at the word. He picked up the slip of paper, letting the ballpoint roll over on its right side, if it had a right side, which he briefly considered was possible but only if you were looking right at the letters **BIC** with the **B** sideways at the top and the **C** sideways at the bottom and only if you assumed that a pen is tall and thin rather than short and very wide.

NADA.

Hubert remembered the day a couple of years ago, December 27th to be exact, when a customer with red suspenders and a white dress shirt rolled up at the sleeves to halfway up the forearms had said to his friend, who was dressed the same except that his suspenders were black, that when you've had bad service the nickel tip is better than no tip because the nickel shows that you've thought about it. Hubert had barely heard him from behind the fake ficus tree, because the man was talking in low tones as if sharing a secret which only a few can know. The man had gone on to explain to his associate that no tip at all can be dismissed as accidental oversight, but a nickel shows exactly what you thought of the service. So does a penny, he'd said, if you don't have a nickel, but don't use a quarter because then the server might just think you're unsuccessful.

Hubert wondered whether the man in the overcoat had ever met the man in the red suspenders.

***

That evening, Hubert turned the pages of the telephone book under the fluorescent light in the kitchenette. He ignored the argument between Hector and Rita in the efficiency next door, because once Rita told Hector that he screwed up again and was tired of him being such a something something loser, Hubert considered that he had heard all of this before, and after all it wasn't any of his business.

There were two Richard W. Coxheads in the telephone book. One was Richard W. Coxhead, Atty. The other was Richard W. Coxhead without the Atty. Hubert considered the likelihood that both Richard W. Coxheads were the Richard W. Coxhead who wore his charcoal overcoat to lunch, and that Richard W. Coxhead was a lawyer. He had also considered that Richard W. Coxhead might be bilingual, but since Hubert knew the meaning of **NADA** and Hubert was not bilingual, Hubert deduced that Richard W. Coxhead might not be bilingual either, which was okay of course, especially when Hector and Rita raised their voices and switched to Espanol whenever it got really heated and Rita yelled "Espanol por favor!".

Hubert stared at the telephone number for Richard W. Coxhead without the Atty. He wondered whether Rhonda would answer. Richard W. and Rhonda. In a nicer world it might have said Richard W. and Rhonda Coxhead and not Richard W. Coxhead in the telephone book. But that was none of his business.

If Rhonda answered, he would ask for Richard W. Coxhead. He didn't want to risk being wrong about Rick, or Rich, or Dick.

He could also ask for the man of the house, but asking for the man of the house makes you sound like you don't know the man of the house, and Hubert felt that he knew Richard W. Coxhead, knew him well, better than Richard W. knew himself, and so he would not ask for the man of the house but rather he would ask for Richard W. Coxhead.

But then he remembered. Familiarity breeds trust. Rick. He should ask for Rick. If Richard W. Coxhead were a banker he might be Rich or even Dick, but probably not Rick. But Rick the lawyer sounded right, and probably had always sounded right to Rhonda.

The phone rang in his ear. It rang again. And again. Then a click.

"Hello?" said a woman's voice.

Hubert cleared his throat nervously. "Hello, Rhonda?"

"Who?"

"This is Hubert. Is the man of the house in?"

"What? The man of the house? Who is this?"

"I mean—I'm sorry. Is Rick available?"

"There's no Rick here. Do you mean Rich? Who *is* this?"

"This is Hubert, Rhonda. I was your server today. At Mia's Café and Grille?"

Hubert wasn't sure why he said it as a question, but he was nervous. After several silent seconds, he thought that the call had been disconnected, because the silence seemed long and loud. But then she spoke.

"I wasn't at Mia's today. And my name isn't Rhonda. Rhonda is Rich's administrative assistant. Why—why are you calling here? Did something happen to Rich?"

"I didn't give them paramount service, Mrs. Coxhead. Today. At Mia's. It was my fault with Rhonda's unsweet tea. I don't know how I missed it."

The woman seemed very quiet. Hubert wondered whether

he had ever served her at Mia's.

"Have you ever been to Mia's, Mrs. Coxhead?"

This time she answered quickly, and quietly.

"I have been to Mia's."

"We pride ourselves on paramount service. I owe Rich. Rhonda too. I was thinking that I could bring a half gallon of unsweet tea to your house so maybe Rhonda could have some and Rich could change the Nada to a—"

"Rich proposed to me at Mia's."

Hubert wasn't sure that Mrs. Coxhead was talking to him. He decided to ask a question, just to check.

"Why did he do that?"

"What?"

"Why did he—"

"Because he loved me! He loved me! He wanted to spend the rest of his, his—"

Suddenly Mrs. Coxhead was crying. Hubert had heard his mother cry just like this when he was a boy. There was a low hum, followed by a staccato of in-breaths, followed again by the low hum, and then sniffles, before starting all over again.

Hubert considered the fake ficus tree and the fake palm tree. "He loved you and he brought you to Mia's? Was that before I started working there?"

"Was that before— why would I know that? Why did you call here?" And the crying set in again. Hubert felt a smidgeon awkward, like he did when he walked into the living room when he was eleven and saw his father giving his mother some what for. At least that's what his father had called it. His mother was crying like Mrs. Coxhead, and his father said during the smacks, "*Look* at him *again* and I'll give *you* some *more* what *for*." And his mother had cried like Mrs. Coxhead. Low hum, bunch of in-breaths with no out-breaths, and then lots of sniffles and then one really big out-breath that also was the start of another long low hum. But neither his mother nor his father had seen him, and he stayed frozen in the foyer with the awkwardness until he figured out he should run outside and play with Starkey White like his dad always told him he should do because Starkey was a good baseball player and Hubert's father wished Hubert could be more like Starkey. *More* like *Starkey.*

Hubert decided that Mrs. Coxhead must want to talk to him, because she was still crying and still on the phone.

"Does Rich speak Spanish, Mrs. Coxhead?"

She stopped sniffling.

"Why would you ask me that?"

"Well. Instead of a number, like dollars and cents, he wrote Nada."

"The word?"

"Yes. It means nothing."

"I know what it means. It means something."

Hubert was confused. He decided to confirm that it means something.

"It means nothing, Mrs. Coxhead."

"It means *everything*. It means he's an asshole. And you have ruined my life by calling me. *Ruined it!* I don't know what to do."

Hubert was unsure why her life was ruined by a telephone call.

"Why have I ruined your life, Mrs. Coxhead?"

"Because my husband is having an affair."

"I ruined your life because your husband is having an affair?" Hubert was terribly confused.

"You ruined my life by telling me."

"I'm sorry, Mrs. Coxhead."

Silence.

"Mrs. Coxhead?"

Silence.

"Mrs. Coxhead, I would like to take this unsweet tea to Rhonda. Do you know where I might find her? I need my gratuity."

"At this hour, who knows where you would find that, that, that—"

"Administrative assistant?"

Silence.

"Maybe I could drop it off at her office. Mrs. Coxhead?"

"He said he was working late. My God, what am I going to do?" She started crying again.

"I have the office address, if Rhonda is Mr. Coxhead's administrative assistant. Maybe I can drop off the unsweet tea there, Mrs. Coxhead. Do you think they will give me my gratuity if I do that? I'm worried about my rent. Failing to provide paramount service cost me a tip, and I need twenty-five tips a day to pay the rent. You see, that's before I pay the power bill. That's five tips a day, just that, Mrs. Coxhead. They let me eat at the restaurant, and three tips a day is for gas in my car. Did you know that my car has gone over two hundred thousand miles, Mrs. Coxhead? Mrs. Coxhead? Mrs. Coxhead, are you okay?"

Hubert heard another sniffle, followed by "I have to go now. I wish you hadn't called. You should have minded your own business."

"This is my business, Mrs. Coxhead."

Silence. Hubert waited for a sniffle. None came. She was gone. Unless she was just testing him. No. She was gone.

Hubert considered going to Mrs. Coxhead's house to see whether she was okay. He didn't want to have ruined her life, since that wasn't his business. But paramount service was. He could leave the unsweet tea at the Coxheads' house with Mrs. Coxhead, and then maybe she could front him the tip if her husband wasn't home. But on the other hand, the tip wasn't her responsibility, and besides, Hubert hadn't earned it yet.

Better to take the unsweet tea directly to Rhonda. Especially if she and Richard W. Coxhead were still working.

***

Hubert parked his rusty old silver Gremlin under a street-light at the corner of Platt Street and Faber Avenue. He walked down the tree-lined street to 811 Faber Avenue, the address of Burke and Coxhead, Attorneys at Law.

Lights were on inside. The front door was closed, but opened with a twist of the knob. He entered. Nobody was in the reception area, so he walked on past the front counter and down the hallway behind it, toward a light emanating from beneath a closed door.

He stopped at the door when he heard music. Soft jazz, it seemed. He touched the handle of the door and turned it. He opened the door and stopped.

Richard W. Coxhead was on top of, it looked like, yes it was, it was Rhonda. His pants were down around his ankles as he appeared to be on the verge of falling off of the desk while somehow staying stuck on the woman. The woman was making noises that Hubert had heard other women make when he watched movies on cable in his efficiency and that one time when that lady from the third red booth asked him if he dated and he said he didn't know and she said she wanted to find out and they went to that place that rented rooms by the hour on Cannon Street.

Hubert decided to take a closer look at Richard W. Coxhead and Rhonda. He especially thought he might be able to help in some way. He owed it to Richard W. Coxhead. And maybe even to Rhonda, though the important thing was that he knew that he owed her a refill of unsweet tea.

He stepped closer. Richard W. Coxhead said something to God. He sounded earnest. The telephone rang.

Hubert said, "I'll get it."

Rhonda screamed as Richard W. Coxhead fell backward onto

his knees and scrambled to his feet. The phone rang again as Hubert kept his promise. He picked up the receiver from the side of the desk and waved at Richard W. Coxhead and Rhonda, nodding his head in reassurance. "I've got it," he said as he raised the phone to his ear. "Don't let me interrupt what you were doing."

"Hello?" he said into the phone as Richard W. Coxhead waved his arms wildly and shook his head back and forth with vigor.

"Rich!" said the voice on the phone. "Why haven't you answered? I've been calling!"

Hubert recognized the voice immediately. "Mrs. Coxhead?" said Hubert, as Rich approached him, mouth wide open and yammering silently, both hands reaching for the phone as Rhonda rolled off of the desk and crawled toward the black leather sofa on the opposite side of the room.

"Mrs. Coxhead?" Hubert said again when he encountered silence at the other end.

Silence. But he heard her breathing. It was coming in short puffs.

"I want to speak with my husband."

Hubert considered that this might not be a good time for Mrs. Coxhead to talk with her husband.

"Mrs. Coxhead, Rich is a bit indisposed at the moment. And I have brought Rhonda her unsweet tea."

Richard W. Coxhead was waving his arms.

"Yes, Rich?"

Richard W. Coxhead stopped waving his arms and whispered, hissed really, "We're working late. Tell her we're working late and I'll be home in about an hour. Tell her!"

Hubert watched Richard W. Coxhead and Rhonda as they got dressed, all four of their hands shaking, sort of like when Hubert was trying to ring up a bill, get more water for a table, and turn in an order to the kitchen, all in ten seconds. It made his hands shake to do everything at once. Richard W. Coxhead was watching Hubert with his head, and trying to put his socks on while pulling up his pants at the same time. Richard W. Coxhead's hands were shaking with the impossibility of putting socks on and pulling pants up at the same time. That was why his hands were shaking.

"Rich wants me to tell you he'll be home in about an hour," Hubert said into the phone. "He and Rhonda are getting dressed."

Hubert didn't see Richard W. Coxhead coming, because he was listening to Mrs. Coxhead, who really did cry a lot for a grown woman. But he did hear him use a swear word as Richard W. Coxhead ripped the phone away from Hubert and then hit Hubert in the head with it. Hubert fell back a couple of steps, and reached up to feel his head, which hurt. His fingers were wet when he withdrew them from his head. The man had hit him right in the spot where his father always did, only this time it wasn't for snorting in church.

The hot sick feeling came back to Hubert's stomach as he listened to Richard W. Coxhead talk into the phone.

"This bastard just barged into my office without notice. We were working on the Carlyle file, and this loon comes in, and get this baby, he was our freaking waiter today, and there's something wrong with him, and I love you, and I can't wait to get home if I can just get the Carlyle file wrapped up here and—"

Hubert shot Richard W. Coxhead with the gun he had used to kill his father twelve years, two months and six days ago. The former Richard W. Coxhead collapsed to the floor, bleeding from his left temple, the phone still in his left hand.

Hubert bent down to pick up the phone. Rhonda screamed, sitting in the corner, hugging herself. Hubert put the phone to his ear.

"I'm sorry, Mrs. Coxhead. I have unsweet tea for Rhonda. I have to go."

Hubert hung up the phone on its base on the desk, and turned toward Rhonda. He removed the unsweet tea from his bag and handed it to her. Her hands were still shaking, because she wasn't finished getting dressed, her face registering what he hoped was gratitude for the refill of unsweet tea, but he wasn't so sure. He wondered whether she would offer the gratuity. Getting no response aside from another scream, he turned to leave.

Service had been delivered. He had remained consistent, just as he had always been. The lady from Florida would have been proud.

Rhonda's voice stopped him. It was a hoarse whisper, but unmistakably Rhonda. Besides, there was nobody else there. Hubert turned.

"Why, Hubert? Why did you do that? Was it—was it the tip?"

Hubert considered the Nada. He considered the man in the red suspenders two years ago. He considered his father. He considered his mother.

"No, Rhonda. It wasn't. I didn't give you paramount service, and Richard W. Coxhead wrote Nada on the check. That's fair, I guess. No ma'am, not the tip."

"Wh—what, then?"

Hubert considered again. He liked Rhonda, even if she did like men who were impossible and embarrassed her and used the same word in a sentence three times. And then he knew.

"It was like the man in the red suspenders said, Rhonda. Leave a nickel, so they'll know you thought about it. I thought about it. Richard W. Coxhead lied to Mrs. Coxhead. He didn't lie to me, and he didn't lie to you. But he lied to Mrs. Coxhead, and so I had to give him some what for."

Hubert stood there and looked at Rhonda.

"Would you like some what for, Rhonda?"

Rhonda stared, mouth agape, around the room, her eyes growing dull as they moved from the desk to the computer to the phone and over toward the outer office and beyond, and then looked at Hubert's eyes. When she spoke, her voice was soft, but firm.

"Yes."

THE CLOSING

❋ ❋ ❋

An excited murmur came to life when the audience was informed of the PhD in Biogenetics, the B.S. in Mechanical Engineering, and then the sweet icing: the minor in English. The minor in English! All of the numbered cards were raised at once. The auctioneer paused and raised his hand, like a teacher calling for quiet.

"Patience, ladies and gentlemen. You will all have opportunities to bid. As I have asked for an opening bid of three hundred thousand and gotten it from all of you, I will simply progress logically to four hundred thousand. Do I hear four hundred thousand?"

All of the numbered cards remained raised. What a relief, Henry almost said aloud from his seat on stage. Dad had been right. The old man had been right all along.

"We will progress again. Do I hear five hundred thousand?"

Henry felt sorry for the bespectacled man in the front row. He was the only bidder to lower his card. The little man's enthusiasm for the combination of science and humanities was obvious and refreshing, but a half million globals was now publicly out of the little man's reach, or that of the corporation which he represented, and so the man adjusted his eyeglasses with both hands, as if that adjustment had caused him to lower his card. Red-faced from embarrassment, the little man packed his notes and his tablet into his purple leather briefcase, made brief eye contact with Henry, and moved toward the side exit.

Everybody knew that bidders were not permitted to remain on site after withdrawal from the process, but still Henry felt sorry for the man. Humiliation among one's peers lays bare one's limitations in ways which matter.

When the bespectacled man had completed his exit, whispers were allowed by the auctioneer for a few seconds, after which he said into the microphone, "If you don't have the cash, you'd best be ready to dash!" The laughter throughout the room lightened the mood, as all were relieved not to be the one with the least, and the bidding resumed with a relaxed confidence in the air.

"For the liquid remaining among us," the auctioneer paused to allow the resumed tittering to subside, "perhaps I should create some separation. Do I hear one million globals?"

Henry admired the auctioneer's command of the value of time. Two thirds of the attendees lowered their numbered cards and packed them into their folders and briefcases. Unlike the bespectacled gentleman, who had no business being at the auction if his corporation couldn't afford eye surgery for its most senior executives, these erstwhile bidders did not look at Henry or anything else as they made their way to the exits. They were not red-faced, for they were not without company. There is no humiliation outside of the loneliness of least. That was, after all, why Henry was here.

Within minutes there were two bidders remaining. One, a white-haired woman of about sixty, clearly owned a majority interest in her corporation. Such was self-evident. The other was a black-haired man in his early thirties, about Henry's age. Henry was impressed that this man had attained bidder status at a human resources auction while still so young. He had obviously gotten started early, had known what he wanted from life, indeed had recognized what life offers to those who can resist pursuing their passions and can avoid other-regarding behavior in both their formative *and* their ladder-climbing years. Yes, Dad had been right. He had been right all along.

This man had obviously listened to his father rather than his mother. Not just when he was twenty-three, as Henry was when he finally began listening to his father's admonishments about the foolishness behind outmoded fantasies like fairness or justice or integrity. No. This man before him, holding firm the card that said 19 on it, had most likely started listening to his father when he was five or six. Young enough to believe his elders, yet old enough to understand that the reason that you believe is that you get something for it. This lesson, when it sticks, lasts a lifetime. Many was the time that Henry had lamented refusing the candy that was offered as reward for cheating on the first addition-and-subtraction test in Second Grade. For this his father had spanked him, albeit only with a folded newspaper. A year later, when Henry failed his science test by ignoring the test answers left on the dry-erase board by the teacher when she left the room for a coffee break, his father had locked him in his room for the entire ensuing weekend. Still Henry had continued to disappoint. But he had wanted to understand, he had said to his father. No, no, no, his father had repeated. This is not about understanding. This is about results.

Now, sitting on the stage and regarding the two remaining bidders, he recognized why he was sitting on the stage, while the woman, clearly an owner, and the young man, clearly a deal-maker, engaged in bidding for the rest of Henry's life.

He wished that his father were still alive to see this. Seven figures for his first son. Seven figures! His father would have been more proud to have the black-haired man be his son, certainly, yes, but still, but still…Henry was amounting to something here. Seven figures. Marian and the children would be provided for. Henry was a Provider now.

A Provider.

Looking at the fifty or sixty years forthcoming as a Provider prior to the month of retirement, a month which the closing documents would guarantee, Henry felt certain that Dad would be proud of him this day. Marian would be able to have the mortgage on AutoPay, perhaps even pay it off before Henry died, although that would of course be a close one. The kids would be able to bypass the waste represented by educational depth, and instead enter a management program at eighteen, as surely the black-haired man in front of him had done. To be on the side of the Bidders, not the Providers—here was wisdom, and Marian would have time now, time to teach the kids everything that had not come naturally to Henry, time to—

In his reverie, Henry had missed the awarding of the winning bid to the black-haired man. The white-haired woman was arguing loudly with the auctioneer, something about a quick clock, but the auctioneer waved for security to come and remove her, which two large men in yellow shirts accomplished gently. Very gently, as they were Providers and she was not.

The black-haired man put his card on his seat and closed his orange briefcase. He approached the stage. Henry rose to shake his hand, to congratulate him and his corporation. After all, they had landed a Ph.D in Biogenetics, a B.S. in Mechanical Engineering, and a minor in English.

The seven figures would work out to about twenty-five thousand globals per year by the time Henry turned eighty-five. If he lasted to ninety, qualifying him for the month's retirement as long as the retirement included the week of the Fourth of July, the black-haired man's investment would indeed be quite impressive. Quite savvy indeed.

The two men shook hands, as men do. They left together to attend the closing in the lawyer's office down the hall. As the black-haired man filled him in, not without enthusiasm, about the dormitory in India and its various amenities, Henry beamed.

Marian would respect him now. He had to imagine that she would. He was providing. For the mortgage (fifty years of it anyway), the TV bills, the texting bills, and probably even the water bills, but water was an extravagance that she needed to get under control. Those blasted water cards. The interest was exorbitant.

And Dad, well, Dad would have wanted this. Amounting to something. That was what it was about, this life, was amounting to something.

As he entered the closing room, Henry began to wonder whether Marian might possibly want a picture of this moment. For the kids. Something to remember their father for. For providing. Providing and amounting to something. He asked the black-haired man about a photograph. Perhaps a pose with the new boss?

"If you get off to a good start, Dr. Hollister. Four weeks, perhaps."

"Just a picture, sir. Mightn't we just have one taken now?"

The man with the black hair looked at Henry. There was displeasure in his eyes. Disappointment even.

"Your wife's mortgage payments will be autopaid for the next fifty years, Dr. Hollister," the black-haired man said.

Henry recognized the overreach.

"I'm sorry, sir."

"Assuming that you reach your productivity goals in each of those six hundred months."

"Naturally. May I ask whether I may see my children again?"

"Of course. Four weeks after you ask for a photograph."

"Four weeks to see them?"

"Four weeks to ask."

"That sounds fair."

"Dr. Hollister."

"Yes, sir?"

"Fair is not a word which we use at Tinhill Corporation. It is not, after all, mission-appropriate."

"What is, sir?"

The black-haired man looked irritated.

"What is what?"

"Mission-appropriate."

The black-haired man pondered the question. He looked at the ceiling. He looked at the floor. He looked at his fingernails. Then light entered his eyes.

"The bottom line, Dr. Hollister. That is mission. That is faith. That is purpose. That is commitment. That is logic."

"That is love?"

"You just lost the fourth week of your retirement. Keep it up, why don't you."

The lawyer, who had busily ignored the conversation between Bidder and Provider, pushed a stack of papers across the table and said "Initial the highlighted areas." Henry reached for the signing pen, sad about the fourth week of his retirement, and put his initials on the first yellow swish.

A GAME OF CHESS

A GAME OF CHESS

✳ ✳ ✳

AUGUST 19TH

Can't think of what to write, but my kid got me this book to write in. So I'll write. Today was the first day of school. I put the flag up at 7:45. A mom said hi after she let her kid out, and said the flag was dirty and that's no way to treat freedom. She drove away along the curb and I didn't say nothing to the back of her vehicle. After that I went out to the soccer field and pulled weeds from the track that goes around it. That was on the list of stuff the business manager wanted me to do before the end of the day, and they said it might rain on the radio this morning. Of course it didn't because I got all the weeds up before ten. If I'd of changed out the washer in the left sink in the boys bathroom first instead of last, it would of started raining cats and dogs right then and never let up. Trust me. Then Mrs. Cutler would of told the business manager the track is a mess and no wonder there's sand gnats and why can't this school do anything right and maybe she would of even told the headmaster. She likes being on the board I think.

I had a tuna fish samwich from the kitchen ladies for lunch. It was good. A kid in line in front of me said there's too much mayo and she wanted a salad instead, but I like mayo and besides I told her she would grow up big and strong if she ate the tuna fish because it has protein. She said mayo is fattening and her mom said the lunch ladies should know that when they make lunch for the students and the big and strong stuff is for the birds. Yikes. The kid's twelve years old and already worried about her figure. Yikes like I said. When I was twelve nobody ever said nothing about saturated fat or nothing like that, and I'm still here after 54 years.

Okay. So I like this thing. Maybe I'll write in it some more tomorrow night just to make Tracy happy. It was for my birthday. She must want me to use it if she's giving me this instead of a Braves game in Atlanta like last year. That was a good game even if the Bravos got beat. I guess now I can go to Atlanta for a game and then come home Sunday night and write about it. Kind of hard now though, because school has started and football games are on Friday nights and I line the field late Friday afternoon for time and a half so the field paint is real bright for the game at 7.

Time for bed. Man. I'm glad I got those weeds done. Got to pull them out by the roots if you want to make things nicer out there. Right out by the roots. Makes better things grow out of the same dirt. Sure does.

AUGUST 20TH

Today the lady who loves flags rolled her window down and said if I don't start taking pride in my country, I might have a real good chance up close to see a shiny clean flag at the government building where they do the unemployment signups. Boy, my old Corps buddies would of cracked up all over the place.

The headmaster came to see me today in the shop. I was fixing a gear in the old tractor so I could haul the trash cans to the Dempsey. That's our dumpster. I just call it the Dempsey. In case somebody reads this besides me some day and doesn't know what the heck I'm talking about. The headmaster keeps saying to call him Bob, but I says I can't because he's a sir. I don't tell him that though. I just says yes sir. When he says call him Bob. Today he leaned up against the tractor. Boy, he looked tired. We talked a little bit about the Braves like we always do and he said Chipper Jones has to stay healthy for once if the Braves are going to go to the playoffs and I says you're right because as Chipper goes the Braves go. And the headmaster says well put and spot on. He likes to say spot on. And boy, does he know his baseball! He's got all them books in his office and everybody wants a piece of him and a piece of his time and a piece of his soul if you ask me but nobody does, but he says he loves baseball as much as anything except his family and everybody's kids because baseball is really fair. He says that a lot when we talk about the Braves and when we played baseball when we was kids and he played in college and I played in the Corps. The fairest game in the world, except for chess, he says.

I ain't never played chess, I says. The headmaster said my gosh and invited me to learn. Said I could learn by playing with him. I says yes sir, and he says please call me Bob and I says yes sir and maybe we'll play chess but I don't say that out loud because I think maybe he's just being nice. Being the headmaster and all.

So today he leans up against that old green tractor and makes a deep breath and breathes out real long, and says do I know Mrs. Tattall and I says no I don't think so. He says Mrs. Tattall likes to complain about teachers usually, but today she sent the headmaster one of them emails where she really lets fly and he said she really likes to let fly. He said it was all about the flag not being crispy and clean. I says I think it's pretty clean sir, and he says I think so too. He says he wrote her back and said he thinks it looks fine and it's up every morning right when school starts and Stan, that's me, Stan does a great job and Stan works for the headmaster not you. I don't mean you if someone reads this some day and doesn't know what the heck I'm talking about. I mean Mrs. Tattall. The lady who loves new flags. I bet she said the school was crapping on freedom but the headmaster didn't say she did but I bet she did.

I almost called him Bob right then but I says thank you sir and he says come see him if I need anything or if I want to play chess some time and I says thank you sir and he says Bob. And he walks out of the shop.

I had the vegetable lasagna today. It was good but I wanted to take a nap about two o'clock.

AUGUST 21ST

Today was the third day of school. The flag lady got out of her car this morning and folded her arms like she was waiting for something. I finished raising the flag to the top of the pole and then I says can I help you because we're supposed to say that. She says she can't imagine how. For the life of her she says. So I start walking to my next project and she yells EXCUSE ME!! And I stopped. I says are you talking to me and she says of course I'm talking to you and maybe I can help her after all by explaining to her why I like to crap on freedom. Well now I started to get mad but I stayed calm and said nothing and she says she told the headmaster yesterday and my days are numbered. I couldn't say nothing no more so I says really? And she says yes for country and freedom and God. And I says, hey, the headmaster says the flag looks just fine and she says really and she says well we'll see about that and then she says maybe the board needs to hear about this.

She went and got back in her big white SUV and drove off, and I went to change out a fluorescent in the chemistry lab.

About four o'clock the headmaster came to see me again. He had a box with him and it was a chess set. He said he's gonna teach me the game and do I want to try and I says I don't clock out till 5 and he says don't worry he won't tell my boss and we laughed. Because he's my boss. In case somebody reads this some day and doesn't know what the heck I'm talking about.

We moved some stuff like loose tools and things and set the board down on top of the table next to the circular saw. He got out the pieces and said there's two sides and they're black and white. He lined up the little pieces and said they were pawns and I said I heard of them before and he showed me where they can go. Two spaces for the first one when you start, but only one after that until the game is all over. I thought that's too bad them pawns only get to go one space at a time when everybody else gets to do lots of moving around as long as they follow the rules like zigzag or sideways or backwards or forwards or two up and one over but not whatever you want because you're not that free, but that queen she gets to go wherever she wants and who made that rule? And your side loses when your king dies.

I don't see much difference between the king and them pawns, being truthful, seeing as how they can both only go one step, except when the king dies everybody on the team dies and when a pawn dies he's just out of everybody's way. Okay, yes. The king can run away if he wants. Real slow, but he can do it if he has help. That's the biggest difference. I guess.

The headmaster said he had a meeting at five o'clock and he didn't want to go but he had to because it was the board and it was a surprise meeting and in ten years they didn't have no surprise meetings and he was glad we got to play chess even though it was just teaching today. And I says thanks for teaching me and I'm gonna see if Tracy wants to play some day if she and whats his name come to visit from Atlanta because the headmaster gave me the chess set when we were done and I said thank you Bob and I took it home with me tonight.

I had the beefaroni for lunch today and a kid carton of chocolate milk. It was good. I wonder how the surprise meeting went for Bob.

AUGUST 22ND

Today I put the flag up real early so I wouldn't see the flag lady. When I was trying to get the air conditioning in the Middle School building to stop making one part of the building feel like Alaska and the other part feel like Miami in July, I started thinking about playing Bob in chess. I wondered if I could beat him some day. Wouldn't that be great. I went to the library last night down on Charles Street, and they had a book about chess strategy and stuff. Wow. But that's nothing. Wait till you hear this if you read this some day like maybe Tracy.

After school ended and the kids all went home except for football and volleyball practice, Bob came to see me in the shed again. We got out the chess set and started playing. He was black and I was white. But that's nothing. Wait till you hear this.

Right out of the blue Bob asks me to teach a class. I says huh? He says yep I want you to teach a class. Says these kids need lessons in manners and the golden rule and how to treat people and he says I'm the guy to teach the class. Well, I reminded Bob that I don't have a degree or nothing or any of those certificates I hear about and he says something like pshaw or something like that and says he still ain't seen no certificate teach a class. Says I got class and class died a long time ago and I says I ain't disagreeing with you about that. About the dying part. And he says then that means you'll teach it and I says really Bob I don't know how to teach. And he says teach who you are, Stan. Teach who you are. Well, my heart starts pounding because Tracy would be real proud of her old man teaching a class at a college prep school where he mows the grass and changes the washers and puts up the flag in the mornings.

So I have to quit writing in this for tonight because I'm doing what Bob called a Prep. I'm doing my Prep for class. I can't believe I start next week! Two classes. One's at 1:15 with 17 freshmen, and the other is at 2:05 with 18 freshmen. How do I Prep for 45 whole minutes with the kids, I asked him. Bob said teach who you are, and then he put me in checkmate. Then he stuck out his hand and I shook it. You know, I've shook his hand a hundred times and I never stopped to think that kids should be taught to shake hands. I see Bob shake hands with kids all the time. I'll tell you what. My students are going to shake hands every day when they see each other in my class. That's how we'll start. With a handshake.

We'll go from there.

The reason Bob put me in checkmate today was because I should of castled. It's right there on page 27. One of these days I'm going to stick my hand out there first, and he'll shake his head at night and say he should of castled and Stan put him in checkmate and shook Bob's hand with class.

I forget what I had for lunch today. It doesn't matter. You don't need to know either, in case somebody's reading this some day and wondering why in the heck it makes any difference if someone else knows what I eat every day. It's not like I got that Twitter thing. So I'm done with that. I've got my Prep to do.

AUGUST 23RD

Today was Friday. I got to the flagpole early again, but she was waiting for me. I don't know where she put her kid so early, because the school doesn't let kids get dropped off before 7:30, but there she was at 7:15 and she had something with her. It was a new flag, all crispy and folded into a triangle just like I fold the school's every day when I get ready to go home. She says do you know what this is and I says yes it's a new flag and she says congratulations you don't need to get your eyes checked and you need to use this flag starting today. I says no thank you. I says our flag has been through a lot right here with

the kids and the teachers and me and Bob. Like when those ter-
rorists attacked New York and we all got together like a family
here at school and cried and said the Pledge of Allegiance to
this flag. THIS flag I says. I says this flag ain't never let us down,
and I ain't going to let her down when she doesn't deserve that
unless Bob says so. And she says do you mean to tell me that
you never replace a dirty filter or old sheets or old clothes or
am I just a slob and I says maybe you weren't listening to what
I just said and she says you impertinent something if this new
flag ain't up by the time school starts in, she looks at her watch
like drama and stuff, in less than thirty minutes then I can take
the old flag home with me. And I says I don't respect threats
and she says facts not threats and so I says I work for Bob and
not her. And she says the headmaster might just be joining you
and she gets in her big white thing and drives off so fast she
don't hear me say what I say to her bumper sticker that says
what would Jesus do.

I know I promised last night I wouldn't write about lunch
but. When I went in the lunch room everybody was talking
about the email. Some teachers came up to me and said way
to go, Stan, that's great. A couple of the guy teachers were
whispering over at the table by the salad bar, and they were
looking at me and I think they were whispering about the
email. I don't think they thought it was great and they didn't
get up and say way to go, Stan, that's great. They laughed
and dipped their rolls in gravy at the same exact time and
shook their heads.

Bob gave me a copy of the email when he came to play
chess this afternoon at 4 o'clock. He said he knows I only use
my box in the faculty lounge and not my email account even
though I have an email account and he says that's okay because he likes going to his box in the faculty lounge too. So I
read the email letter and it was real good because Bob wrote

it to all the teachers and parents and the students who are old enough to have email accounts. He said freshmen are going to have one study hall instead of 2, and they're going to take a class with me. Me! Stan Howland! I still can't believe it and he said they're going to learn ethics and class and manners and the importance of respect and the golden rule from Mister Howland and not Stan. He didn't say not Stan but I want you to understand in case you're not Tracy and you're reading this one day and don't know what the heck I'm talking about. Bob's email says this is part of becoming a quality human being and it's one of the reasons the school is here and we shouldn't forget that and it's not about test scores but being educated and complete and Mister Howland will be part of helping kids become complete. I got the email letter right here. That's what it says.

Mister Howland.

This weekend I'm going to do three things. Fix the shed floorboard so I can put my lawnmower back in there before it gets rained on again. Two: Watch the Bravos play the Phillies and man I hope Chipper's hamstring feels better and three: Do my Prep for Monday. Bob says the class is called How To Be. How to be. That seems real simple to me. I hope I can fill up the 45 minutes all year but I bet I can. I got lots of stories too, and I bet the kids do too. I got to learn how to give grades though. I hope I don't need a certificate for that but Bob says I don't and Bob says he ain't never seen a certificate give no grade. I don't think Bob cares about certificates.

Kind of nervous, got to admit. But I remember my football coach in high school telling me if you're nervous that's good because it means it's important to you and that means you're ready and you're passionate. I hope Coach Deaton and Bob are both right even though Coach Deaton didn't coach no more after we went 2 and 8 my senior year.

AUGUST 24TH

The floorboard's done. The mower's back inside the shed. So now it won't rain for three weeks. Right? Well, at least it won't get stolen.

The Bravos lost, 4 to 1. Chipper didn't play. Those hamstrings. Man. I hope I don't tweak one. Funny they say tweak nowadays. When I tweak something at my job, it's to make it work better. But Chipper's hamstring is tweaked, and it's a bad thing all right. No tweaks for me. I can't afford to miss work. Don't have that Yogi Berra insurance with the duck.

AUGUST 25TH

Sundays always make me feel strange. I should be glad I have the day off, but it's like I can see Monday waiting for me. Monday is a big white vehicle with a brand new crispy flag on it. I still like the old one. We've been through a lot together. You never know what Monday will bring. But I know one thing. Today I'm doing my Prep. I'm a Teacher now. A Faculty Member. Mister Howland.

I'm back. It took me three hours, but. Tomorrow I'm going to talk to the kids about How To Be. Bob says there's 36 weeks in the school calendar. So. We're going to learn 35 ways to be. 35 not 36 because one week's already done and if kids get good at 35 then I guess I've done a pretty good job with those freshmen. I don't have a certificate, but. I know 35 ways to be. Maybe we'll start with Mrs. Tattall. First, kids, don't be like the flag lady. I'm just kidding, in case you think I would tell the kids not to be like the flag lady. I would tell the kids not to be like the flag lady, but some of them probably don't know who Mrs. Tattall is or even care and I don't blame them because Mrs. Tattall is my problem and not theirs and maybe Bob's problem and I think yeah she's Bob's problem too. And also. If you think about it, if you tell them not to be like the flag lady, then really you're being like the flag lady. Aren't you.

35 ways to be. That's the plan. A week for every way to be. That also gives time to fit in 35 ways not to be, right?

I forgot Tracy's calling tonight. Bye. Gotta answer.

AUGUST 26TH

Well, I don't know where to begin. The flag lady or Tommy Cutler or Bob. Or. I'll start with the flag lady. So she pulls up like usual in the big white thing, but this time she has a camera. She takes a picture of me putting up the flag, then she puts the camera away and gets out another one and this one's a video camera. She makes a production of opening it up and turning it on and then points it at me when I'm trying to wrap the cord around the hook at the bottom of the pole. I says what's the movie for and she says for recording your disrespect and I says okay and I start to walk away and she says real loud see what I mean. I stop and say to the camera that it's not disrespectful to do my job and she says how about when you suddenly get to be a teacher when you haven't earned it and I say and I shouldn't have said it but I say Bob thinks I've earned it and she says Bob has no respect for the flag or the kids if he thinks a dirty flag and a janitor are good enough for the pole and the classroom and that's why he's done. And I say who's done and she says the headmaster and she turns off the camera and gets in her giant white Yeti and drives off.

So I think well she likes to be dramatic and I pretend not to notice all the stares that day and I show up early for my class in room 114. I was ready too. We were going to talk about the Golden Rule but not like Sunday school class. I had this grade book Miss Denton gave me to write all the kids names in which I did yesterday. The kids come in and two of them are late and I says you're late and they says so what. One of them says it first then the other one says it. So what if we're late. I says that's not How To Be and I say not to worry because that's not how you'll be very soon and one of them says don't worry Stan we won't be late again because this class ain't going to be a class. I says what's your name and he says Tommy Cutler and he says his mom says I'm not his teacher no way no how. I says my name is Mister Howland not Stan and he says you're Stan the janitor and I says Tommy you and I are going to work together pulling weeds after school today, and every day this week. Don't call me by my first name again unless I invite you to, and sit down. Tommy sits down and it's like you can hear a pin drop. Tommy takes out a cell phone, one of them i-phones I think, and starts punching in some stuff. I walk over and take it away and I takes him to the window and I say see those bushes right there and he shrugs and nods his head and I says, You're pulling all the weeds around those bushes, Get to work. He says you can't make me it's hot and I might get dehydrated and then my mom will sue the school and she's on the board so you better stop this right now and I open the door and he looks at everybody and I look at everybody and he goes out and I close the door and everybody watches him sit down like an Indian and he pulls a weed and throws it at the door but then he pulls another weed and puts it down next to his feet and then another and then I said is everybody okay with me being their How To Be teacher and they say yes and I say I promise they won't be bored if they promise to think a little bit about How To Be and I walk around the room and ask everybody their name and I shake everybody's hands and they look at each other and look out the window and I look out the window and Tommy Cutler's not out there. I almost went to the bathroom in my pants.

So I went out the door then went back in and said we're all going out to look for Tommy because we're a community. The kids liked that a lot, so we all went out and I said no yelling just stay close to me and tell me if you see Tommy and pretty quick I heard little Tamera Johnson say there he is. We all looked where Tamera pointed and there he was. Sitting on a picnic table in the quad. We get to the table and I says Tommy and he says yeah and I says we're going to have class right here in the quad and he says I don't care and I says move over and I sit next to him and tell everybody to sit at the table or on the ground or move another table over and four of the kids move another table over and now we've got room for everyone. When everyone is quiet I says we're gonna start the How to Be class with a question. Nobody asks what the question is so I says here's the question. Who thinks that if they were the teacher, they would think Tommy's been doing the right things for the last ten minutes of his life. Nobody said anything, just looked at each other and me. I says just raise your hand if you think Tommy's been doing the right thing today. Nobody raises their hand. I says Tommy you can raise your hand especially if you're proud of yourself or maybe proud of just one thing you've done in the last ten minutes. Tommy doesn't raise his hand. I says hey everyone I have an idea. Tamera Johnson and Freddy Kimball say what's the idea, and I feel Tommy Cutler sort of move a little bit like he wants to know the idea too. I says if everyone can write a good paragraph about why they didn't raise their hand, and that means everyone, then Tommy won't have to go to the headmaster. I could see they liked that idea, because first Tamera and then Freddy and then everybody, even Tommy, gets up and starts running across the quad toward our classroom and I says walk don't run and they walk fast like they can't wait to start. Tommy walks with me. I couldn't believe it. Right next to me. I says Tommy are you going to write a paragraph? He says no sir, I don't know why I didn't raise my hand so I can't write about it. I says maybe you don't know why you didn't raise your hand because it was you that we were talking about and he says yeah I guess so and I says I'm proud of him for not raising his hand and he says but I would have if they had and I says if you know that then you've got something to write about. And he looks at me. Just looks at me. He says can I have my cell phone back if I write the paragraph and I says no and he says okay. I says he can have it back tomorrow if he has a good day tomorrow and I says do you think that's fair and he says yes that's fair.

The paragraphs were pretty good. When the kids were done we read our paragraphs out loud until the bell rang. One kid's paragraph, I don't know his name by heart yet, said he was writing his paragraph so that Tommy wouldn't get in trouble with the headmaster and no other reason and everybody laughed and I said way to go. And some of the kids said What? And I said way to go, you fulfilled a responsibility and helped a friend all at the same time and you were honest about it without being a jackass, and they laughed and whispered to each other that Mister Howland said jackass. And I said tonight your homework is to write a paragraph about not being a jackass. I looked around the room and saw Tommy Cutler. He was packing his bookbag. He didn't read his paragraph to the class before the bell rang, but that's okay. We just ran out of time.

At four o'clock Bob came to the shop and we opened the chess set and set the pieces out and he made the first move and he said he got an email from Mrs. Cutler that she and her lawyer wanted to see Bob first thing tomorrow morning. He had a frown on his face as he took his right forefinger off the top of his pawn, meaning it was my turn. I says is it about our class today? How to Be? And he says yes. I says I had to teach Tommy and the class some things right away and he says Did you call Tommy Cutler a jackass and I says heavens no Bob and I moved my second pawn from the left up one space. He says did you take his cell phone away from him and I says yes and he says good. He says did you give it back and I says no not till tomorrow if he has a good day tomorrow and Bob says good. He says did you call Tommy a jackass and I says no Bob I didn't call him a jackass no. I says I told the kids to write a paragraph tonight about not being a jackass and he says good that's innovative and I says really? And he says yes. He says and you didn't call Tommy Cutler a jackass and I says I swear on my mother's grave and he says that's good enough for him and he moves his bishop out and I know what that means. Time to use what I've learned from the library book.

Bob beat me again, but I got my hand out there first. He looked real sad when I shook his hand. He said he was proud of me, that he looked up to me, and he wished that he had always been more like me. Well, it was a real awkward moment let me tell you. I said thank you Bob that means a lot and it does and he says he wants to give me my new contract and I says new contract and he says why yes you have more responsibilities now and you've had a great first day and I says but you're meeting with Mrs. Cutler tomorrow morning with her lawyer and he says yes why do you think I wanted this How To Be class here, and I says oh I see and he says that poor kid has dinner every night with that lady and it's hard to blame him so we got to help him or we're not really a school and I says exactly. He says my new contract will have an extra ten thousand dollars in it and I says my gosh and he says here it is and he pulls out a folded piece of paper that says Addendum to Stan Howland's Contract and he says sign down here and I take his black pen and I sign it. I sign a second one too. He stands up and says You never know. He waves the contracts in the air when he says You never know, and he looks like he's going to cry. And he gives me one of them contracts to take home with me. I didn't like that. I should of just shook his hand and said you can give me the money on a handshake Bob but I didn't. I kind of think I didn't because of what the flag lady said this morning. About Bob. About what if he's not here to give me the money on a handshake and I think is that why he brought the contract to our chess game and still I should of said no Bob a handshake will do and that's how we should teach kids to be.

I don't feel like sleeping tonight.

AUGUST 27TH

This morning I got to the flagpole and two ladies were waiting for me. The flag lady and Mrs. Cutler. The flag lady went first and said this is your last day Stan. I said Mister Howland and she laughed. I said I only take my orders or my walking papers from Bob. That's when Mrs. Cutler said she, Mrs. Cutler, was this thing called interim head. I said interim head? And she said interim head and said Stan I'm acting under my authority in removing you as an employee at this school as maintenance director and in this little charade as a teacher. I think she said ludicrous or something like that, but she also said little charade so that's what she said. I says what happened to Bob and the flag lady starts to answer but Mrs. Cutler waves her hand like she's stopping traffic and the flag lady shuts up. Mrs. Cutler says I speak for the board Stan when I say that the headmaster has resigned. For personal reasons she said. To pursue other opportunities she said and I said is that a personal reason and she said is what a personal reason and I said to pursue other opportunities and she said it doesn't matter so go pack up your things in the shop and there will be three weeks severance for you and that's very nice of us because this is a right-to-work state and what that means is we don't have to give you a thing Stan but we are. Now my heart is going real fast and kind of booming in my head. I looked at the flag in my hands and thought about saying something pretty not nice but Tracy got me this book so I could have an outlet for my anger, that's what she called it, and I remembered that and then I remembered castling. I remembered castling. You got to remember castling before they get you in checkmate. That's what it said on page 27.

I have a contract, I said. Excuse me Mrs. Cutler asked real loud. I said I have a contract and it says I get extra money for teaching my How to Be classes to freshmen, and it says I am Director of Maintenance. It's an addendum I says. Signed by Bob and me and not just a handshake either. The flag lady says Bob's not the headmaster any more and never will be and Mrs. Cutler stops traffic again and the flag lady shuts up and Mrs. Cutler says Bob's not the headmaster any more and it's unfortunate what happened and I says I think he was the headmaster when he signed it and she says listen if you want your severance then you'll go quietly before the students see you and expect to see you in class. I says is this about the flag or is this about teaching your children not to be jackasses. Their jaws both open up and get stuck. I says now I have to do my job and then get ready to teach your children not to be jackasses and I'm pretty sure they don't want to be jackasses if they can help it. I walked away and then all I could think about was Bob.

I couldn't eat my lunch. I went to the administration building and asked the front desk lady is Bob here and she looked nervous and said no and I says will he be here and she says no and I says can I have his number so I can call him and she says my God Stan I'm so sorry you haven't heard and I say yes I have and she says no you haven't and I says what do you mean and she says Oh My God and puts her hand on her mouth. She says Bob's wife found him a little while ago and

AUGUST 28TH

I can't write today. Sorry, Tracy.

AUGUST 29TH

Sorry.

AUGUST 30TH

Bob was my best friend. We used to play chess together every afternoon, you know. I have to tell you, I don't understand what the flag lady was doing at Bob's memorial service today. Mrs. Cutler neither. Mrs. Cutler even got to speak to the whole audience about the board's great respect for the man and his legacy. That's what she actually said. The man and his legacy. She actually said that, right before she talked about the sad mysteries of depression, and what it can do to great men like Bob. Bob's grown-up son and daughter were in the front row with their mother, thinking how great it is that this wonderful woman is honoring their dad. The man and his legacy. She actually said that. Might as well have been the flag lady up there. Crispy and clean. What a jackass.

Tomorrow my How to Be class and I are going to talk about that word. Legacy not jackass. We're done with jackass. The grownups will keep showing the kids what that is. Since some of the kids went to Bob's service with their parents, I had the kids look up legacy for homework this weekend and use it in a smart sentence in their journals, now that they have one and I have one.

I'm glad Bob and page 27 taught me how to castle. My lawyer says we might have to worry about next year, but that's next year and there's plenty of time for my queen to get busy now that I did my castling. I'm going to send my queen all over that board before next year, and these kids aren't going to be pawns when they grow up. Aren't going to be jackasses neither. Bob saw to that.

There aren't a lot of ways to teach sportsmanship and fairness in a classroom, but those are two of the 35. So. The kids take turns using Bob's chess set. Two kids every class period, no matter what topic we're doing that week. Started two days ago. Today was the first time I saw the loser stick his hand out first.

That's class, Tommy, I says. Real class.

I like to see kids smile when they think you're not looking. That's a quote from Bob.

Spot on, Bob.

SIXTH PERIOD

"Come in!" echoes the voice from the other side.

Robin Tyree opens the heavy oak door, in no hurry to see Mr. Pickard, but nonetheless ready to get it over with.

He doesn't get up from his perch behind the enormous mahogany desk. She closes the door behind her. The click ricochets around the room.

"Mr. Pickard," she breathes nervously. "I really don't have much time. The kids'll only be on afternoon break for ten minutes."

"Sit down, Robin. This will only take five." The squat, balding headmaster smiles briefly, then waves a black flair pen toward a gray vinyl swivel chair placed uncomfortably in the middle of the room.

Robin sits down and commences gushing.

"Mr. Pickard, I really think I have the right to—"

"*Miss* Tyree, you have no right, whatsoever, to contradict an act of Congress. None. You are breaking the law, and exposing this school to unwanted attention and liability, and I will see you *stop*."

"But Mr. Pickard, it was one class day. Just one day. Yes, it was on the seven deadly sins, but we were studying the historical aspect of each in various societies and cultures. I consider it a nondenominational topic, so—"

"Next week it becomes six, Miss Tyree." The headmaster

turns to his computer. "This is not news to you. You received my memo three weeks ago." Mr. Pickard leans over and clicks the mouse on his computer. "I have the receipt."

Screw your receipt, you little...

"Mr. Pickard, we're an independent school," Robin offers, ignoring a vague warning rising from her abdomen. "I'm a teacher at an *independent* school. If I tell my students that greed is not at least historically regarded as one of the deadly sins, what do I imply?"

"You imply that avarice is a virtue, Miss Tyree. Avarice is a virtue. Greed has been removed by law from the English language, in accordance with the Jones-Yawley Act. You will use the word 'avarice' around our students, and you will refer to it as a virtue."

Mr. Pickard leans forward in his best-known method of intimidation.

"And you will hopefully develop some respect for my thirty-one years in *independent* schools, Miss Tyree. One thing I have learned in my career is that the word 'independent' is a dangerous one to embrace too passionately. Now, have you ignored my memo, Miss Tyree, or do you somehow fail to grasp the part of Jones-Yawley which specifically states that teachers, public or private, are no longer permitted to make reference to deadly sins numbering seven. No reference to greed is permitted, except for college philosophy classes, which are grandfathered for three years, through the 2050-51 school year." Mr. Pickard smiles, but his eyes remain riveted on Robin's. "You do not teach a college philosophy class, do you, Miss Tyree?"

Mr. Pickard takes a slow sip of his coffee, then continues.

"Robin, it is decidedly not up to you to teach in violation of the law. Our nation was built on avarice, as Jones-Yawley makes clear. The acquisition of wealth has led to the building of churches, museums, parks, and many other philanthropically-granted sites. Like it or not, Robin, this country, this world, is run by corporations and wealthy individuals. Congress has simply recognized a long-existing truth: Our nation needs to continue to foster avarice among our most talented and intelligent young. Anything that attaches guilt to the pursuit of great wealth has the potential to erode that which our country was built upon. Therefore, outdated and erroneous notions suggesting to children that there are ideals, other than one's own family, greater than the acquisition of money will *not* be tolerated at this school. These children's parents have invested a significant sum for a Chesterton education, and we will not let them down. Am I understood, Miss Tyree?"

"If—if I could just explain what I was trying to do, I—"

Mr. Pickard displays his right palm, like a traffic officer. Robin freezes her sentence. Mr. Pickard rises and gestures toward the door.

"Afternoon break is nearly over, Miss Tyree. Please resume your more responsible work with our students."

Robin wobbles to her feet. She leaves without a word, trying not to hear the click of the door as she shuts it gingerly. She turns and passes a portrait of L. Frank Yardley, founding headmaster of Chesterton, warmly welcoming a young child through the stone portals of the main building a century ago.

Rattled, Robin looks at her watch, smoothes her skirt, wipes a slight trace of moisture from her forehead, takes a deep breath, exhales, and wears what she knows is an unconvincing smile as she hurries down the long west hallway toward her classroom. The hallway is crowded with between-classes students. Several seniors gaze upon her with what Robin is suddenly sure is a derisive and knowing silence, certain to be followed by snickers after she passes.

She catches up with her class, seventeen energetic freshmen, as they file into her classroom for free-reading. She watches her students settle properly into their seats. They withdraw their reading tablets with library respect (just as she instructed them on Rules and Expectations Day during week one).

Certain that her face is flushed red, and unsure whether the blush is from her fear or from her shame at her fear, she thanks herself for scheduling today for free-reading.

Robin pulls her own free-reading tablet from her top desk drawer. She pretends to focus on page fifty-seven of Frank Fettis's new biography of Stephen Torvell, the first man to walk on Mars. She had thought it would be fascinating, indeed inspiring. But the news yesterday, that Torvell signed a lucrative contract to appear on Burger King soda cups, wrestling over a Whopper with the little black-clad Martian from the twentieth-century Bugs Bunny cartoons, has somewhat diminished her curiosity about the shaping of this man's life.

A tittering from the back of the classroom yanks her eyes from page fifty-seven to the desks in the back right corner. There can be no question that Marvin Lyall has again begun free-reading with the exhibition of a humorous drawing to his neighbors. Time to relieve him of the artwork, regardless of how much Robin likes Marvin and his original mind.

Robin stands, noisily sliding her chair legs along the tile floor for effect. The tittering stops. All eyes in the rear corner are re-directed seriously upon electronic pages.

"Mister Lyall," Robin calls firmly.

Marvin, a rather handsome fourteen-year-old in spite of his battle with teenage acne, looks up innocently from his tablet.

"Yes, ma'am?"

"We would all be grateful, as usual, if you would share your art with the class."

This request has become, in Robin's mind, a healthy diversion during the several weeks heading into Holiday Consumption break. After all, Marvin is revered by his classmates, and his drawings seldom stray into subjects or depictions which are distasteful or even unintelligent. A good laugh is usually had by everyone, and the ensuing half-hour generally produces uninterrupted reading by the entire class.

"Yes, ma'am," Marvin replies with expected eagerness, and he produces a yellow lined sheet of paper with today's picture. He turns it out toward the front of the class, for everyone to see.

The drawing depicts a white boy and a black man sitting together on a raft, floating down a river. Marvin has drawn dialogue balloons above both characters, but Robin has to take a few steps toward the back of the classroom in order to see the words uttered by the boy and the man in the cartoon. As she draws near, she sees that the drawings are excellent renderings of Huckleberry Finn and slave Jim from Mark Twain's classic novel of nearly two hundred years ago.

Huck, looking downriver, asks, in Marvin Lyall's signature block writing, "So, Jim, what do you plan to do with your newfound freedom?"

Jim, also peering downriver, replies, "I's goin' ta take Mistah Hen'rickson's salesmanship class at Chessahton Prepatarah Skoo. Gonna lern me to close the Deal of Life. Jes' like Mistah Hen'rickson say. Yessah, I's goin' ta be a closah."

As the children finish reading Marvin's artistic offering, Robin scans the faces in the room. Some, not finding humor in the picture, turn and resume their reading. Marvin's best friends and desk neighbors, David Turner and Juan Ramirez, continue to enjoy a chuckle at Mr. Hendrickson's expense.

Robin, thinking back five minutes to her call to Mr. Pickard's carpet, decides to move the class into discussion of Marvin's cartoon. After all, she has a mortgage to pay.

"Class, let's talk about Marvin's picture today."

All of the students dutifully place their tablets face down on their desks.

"Carolyn," Robin says softly to a shy brown-haired girl in the front row. "You didn't seem to like Marvin's cartoon today. What would you like to say about it?"

Carolyn clears her throat nervously and lowers her head, embarrassed. "It's...It's..." Carolyn mumbles something inaudible to complete her observation.

"Carolyn, please speak up. We couldn't hear you," Robin says, choosing a patient tone.

The girl raises her head, revealing a deep blush.

"It's dirty."

Again the girl looks down to examine her skirt.

Juan Ramirez wastes no time in rising to the defense of his friend's work. "It ain't dirty! Mr. Hendrickson *sucks*." Juan, realizing his mistake, shoots an apologetic look at his teacher.

"I'm sorry, Miss Tyree. It—is—not—dirty," he says hesitantly, as if trying to speak Russian.

"That's much better, Juan. Much better. You're getting it."

As Juan sits up proudly in his seat, forgetting for the moment why he has spoken in the first place, Robin distantly remembers a time, seven or eight years ago, when she might also have expected Juan to amend his unkind remark about Mr. Hendrickson. But over time she has followed school directives to soften her approach to non-academic teaching, to reflect the reality that a capacity for cruelty is essential in a young person's development into a revenue-producing corporate citizen. "Especially at a preparatory institution like Chesterton," the school's trustees made clear when they revised the school's mission statement back in 'forty-one.

She is curious, though, to get at Marvin's purpose in drawing his cartoon.

"Why do you think it's dirty, Carolyn?"

The girl speaks without looking up. "Do I have to?"

"We'd like you to," replies Robin, smiling into the words to encourage Carolyn to develop her willingness to elaborate.

Again the blushing face. "It's kind of, well, bad to talk bad about selling," the girl manages.

"Okay, Carolyn. Thank you. Marvin? Would you like to address Carolyn's comment?"

Marvin leans back confidently. "Yes, ma'am. See, it's like you said about the seven deadly sins. Greed makes selling predatory. I—"

"I didn't say that, Marvin."

The words come to Robin's own ears as if out of a nap dream. Surreal. She almost wheels around to see who uttered them.

Marvin stares back at Robin expectantly, as if waiting for the punch line. "Yes, ma'am. You did too. You said greed is one of the deadly sins because it makes, you know, good people do things they wouldn't ordinarily do. You know, as good people. So, in my cartoon, Jim is already planning to be a closer as a free man. A real good salesman. A corporate carnivore, like Mr. Hendrickson teaches us in Salesmanship."

"Real-*lee* good, Marvin," Robin replies, trying to divert attention from her lie.

"Thank you, ma'am."

"No, Marvin, I mean 'really good salesman'. Real is an adjective, not an adverb."

"Oh, yeah. Right, ma'am. Really right. So anyway, I hate Salesmanship class. It's boring. And I think what you said yesterday about greed was right on, Miss Tyree. I don't want to be a carnivore." Marvin leans forward intently. "I want to be free of avarice."

Robin feels a twinge of guilt as she thinks of her new mortgage payment. Mr. Pickard will be preparing teaching contracts not long after Holiday Consumption break. She **has** to renew her contract. The house has been a long time in coming.

"Why, Marvin, I, I think you misunderstood me. Some of you

might have misunderstood me. You see, Congress just passed a new law that says that there are six deadly sins, not seven. It's called the Jones-Yawley Act. I was wrong when I forgot that. You see, our nation was built on avarice. You—you can see that, can't you?"

Please, God. Just let this drop. These kids can read me like a tablet.

Marvin pushes back his chair and stands up, stunned. "Miss Tyree, how can you *say* that? You sound like my dad. Yesterday you said it was okay to *make* a lot of money, but not okay to *define* your life and success by it. You *said* it was fine to see money as a way to provide for others, like family, but not as a reason to downsize other families' breadwinners for the sake of stock prices. Greed does these things, you said. You also said that—"

"I'm aware of what I said, Marvin. It was only twenty-four hours ago. It doesn't need regurgitation. But I was wrong. I just didn't consider that the people in Washington have access to lots more research than we do, and —"

"In *fact*, Miss Tyree, you told us that we will one day have power over others, as graduates of Chesterton. That words like compassion have grown weak and meaningless. That greed makes us cruel, and that cruel used to be undesirable. That honor and decency and kindness will disappear unless our generation exercises power less selfishly than yours and the ones before yours. You *said*, Miss Tyree," and Marvin pauses and peers aggressively around the room at his classmates, "that all members of our species are hypocrites by nature, and that that's fine as long as we recognize it. That hypocrisy is a matter of degree, that we should keep our hypocrisies small and trivial and unharmful. That the golden rule should be first when we choose or don't choose actions or decisions which affect others. And *now* you say that just because Congress comes up with some stupid Jones-Pawley Act—"

"Yawley!" exclaims Sarah Burnham, three aisles to Marvin's right.

Marvin rolls his eyes and mutters, "So sorry, Sarah. Yawley."

Robin feels the eyes of the classroom riveted upon her. She has been challenged before, almost always by Marvin Lyall, and she has always relished his intellectual courage. He is right, and yet here she stands with a clear directive from her boss that she must reverse herself on a character issue which has conferred upon her the status of dinosaur as an educator.

Marvin combs the fingers of his right hand through his oily hair and sits down. He crosses his legs and folds his arms, regarding his speechless teacher coolly as Robin struggles for the right comeback.

She is too late.

"Excuse me, Miss Tyree," Marvin breathes softly but audibly, "but you're obviously covering your...behind."

The room explodes in nervous but uninhibited laughter. Marvin has never gone this far. No one was prepared for it, and so they laugh, wide-eyed, eyes on Marvin and then, the hilarity dying down, eyes returning cautiously to Robin.

The eyes have changed. Marvin has exposed her in minutes. All good teachers privately harbor worries of being exposed as frauds. It is part of what makes them good teachers, and is part of what ensures that they will never suffer such a nightmare. Robin stares stupidly at Marvin, wishing to somehow intimidate, as her mind races to grab the rope that will pull the departing ship back to harbor.

Scanning the room, she recognizes that she has lost the group. She decides to exercise the obvious, to dismiss Marvin for being disrespectful. She sends him to the dean's office. Marvin slams the door behind him. Robin instructs the class to resume free reading, but now she could swear that even shy little Carolyn Pelham is smiling derisively at the screen of her tablet.

She has lost them.

At the end of the class period, the students seem to rush from the room, most of them having packed their tablets into their bags with a couple of minutes to spare. Normally, Robin would not tolerate such clock-watching behavior, but she wants them out as much as they do.

Robin rises from her desk. She hears a commotion out in the hall, exceeding the normal hubbub between classes. She enters the hall, and is almost run over by colleague Jack Hatfield, who is in a virtual sprint eastward toward the administrative offices.

"Jack!" Robin yells, alarmed.

Jack clops to a stop, and turns. "Yes, Robin," he rasps impatiently, swinging his arms back and forth as if needing to visit the bathroom.

"What's—what's going on?" Robin asks intently.

Jack nervously smooths the hair on the back of his head. "It's one of my advisees. Marvin Lyall."

"Marvin? What's happened?"

"Apparently...well...apparently he drew a derogatory picture of the headmaster and the board, while waiting to see the dean. Somebody kicked him out of class last period, I think, and he made a mistake in the dean's office with one of his damned drawings. That's all I know." Jack turns and resumes his sprint. "I've got to get there!" he calls over his shoulder as he weaves in and out of student traffic. "Got to try to keep him from being expelled!"

Robin stares at the waxed checkerboard floor and begins a slow walk in the direction of the administrative offices. She arrives minutes later outside the headmaster's office and knocks methodically.

The heavy oak door opens to reveal Mr. Pickard's secretary, a grandmotherly woman named Martha West, whom Robin has always liked. Beyond Martha, sitting in the gray vinyl chair in the middle of the room, is Marvin Lyall, his profile appearing tall and straight and confident as he faces the imposing desk of

Mr. Pickard. Jack Hatfield, breathing heavily, is leaning down next to Marvin, a hand on Marvin's right shoulder. Sitting on a sofa under the picture window that overlooks the quad are Marvin's parents. His mother is crying, dabbing at her eyes with a tissue. His father stares at his own shoes.

Mr. Pickard is peering out the window. His pose is pensive, grave. His right hand grips his chin as he turns to face Robin. Suddenly he smiles broadly.

"Miss Tyree. Many thanks for dropping in." The smile disappears, and he puts his hands in his pockets as he paces in front of the window. "Marvin has been telling us an interesting story about you."

Robin's stomach churns with apprehension.

Mr. Pickard heaves a sigh and extends his hand. Robin takes it, hesitating. "I'm grateful to you, Miss Tyree, for defending both myself and the board of trustees, and for taking a painful but necessary step in endeavoring to educate an erring young person. Obviously you were listening this afternoon. You are a fine teacher, and clearly have the capacity to combine creativity with pedagogy in accomplishing our school's mission. I should not have doubted you."

Robin looks quizzically at Marvin, who smiles at her for no good reason at all.

"Miss Tyree, Marvin has told us about the test. Brilliant, is all I can say. You caught Marvin, yes. But you affirmed that most of our students are learning what they need to know in this world. Marvin has admitted that he is not Chesterton material after all, and will voluntarily be attending another school on Monday. But more importantly, what has been confirmed today is that with teachers like yourself leading the way, our school can remain true to our mission statement."

Mr. Pickard pauses and stares at Marvin. "Marvin, would you like to repeat the compliment you paid to Miss Tyree a few minutes ago? It certainly provides evidence that you will be okay eventually, Marvin. Eventually you will paint no pictures that will get you into trouble, and I'm glad that you recognize Miss Tyree's role in your education. Please share what you said a few minutes ago, with Miss Tyree."

Marvin swivels in the gray vinyl chair to face Robin.

"Sure, Mr. Pickard," Marvin says positively, not taking his eyes off of Robin. "Miss Tyree, what I said was that if you had been my teacher all along and not just now, I would be a model Chesterton student. I will try to remember your example in my attempt to right myself at another school."

"And I'm sure you will, Marvin," says Mr. Pickard just as positively, and claps his hands to signify that all is finished and fileable. "I'm sure you will."

Minutes later, all but Mr. Pickard have exited the headmaster's office. Robin, shaken, heads for her car, an old gray '38 Volvo moored in the back parking lot next to a student's late-model Mercedes-Benz. She places her forehead against the steering wheel for several long seconds, reviewing her career, dreading tomorrow, dreading the quiz she would write tonight, dreading her weekly text conversation with her parents.

She lifts her head and adjusts the rearview mirror. Gravely, she opens the glove compartment and removes several items until she finds what she is looking for. She scribbles on a small rectangular sheet of paper. She scribbles on another small rectangular sheet of paper. She tears the second sheet of paper from its pad. She looks at herself in the mirror. She brushes her fingers through her hair unnecessarily. She takes both small pieces of paper and places them in an envelope.

Sighing, she starts the car and pulls out of the parking lot and heads southward on Chesterton Avenue. She arrives minutes later at the Publix shopping center. She locates the driveup mail-drop, and pulls alongside. Glancing again at the rearview mirror, she again adjusts it, to give her a better look at what is behind her.

Satisfied with the adjustment, Robin Tyree drops her mortgage payment in the "Out-of-Town" box and pulls back into the center's traffic, glancing at her watch to see that, indeed, she has plenty of time until the day's last period.

THE GUEST

* * *

The answering machine down the hall in the kitchen clicked on after the fourth ring. Carl stared warily at the portable phone atop the dust-blanketed printer, ready to answer, maybe, if the caller wasn't from the home office. He waited for Rachel's tired voice to finish the greeting.

The machine beeped.

"Carl, it's me." Her voice wafted from the kitchen, attractive but irritating in its "I-know-what-you're-doing" kind of way. "Pick up, honey. It's about dinner."

Carl heaved himself out of his black swivel desk chair, sighed heavily, and picked up the portable.

"Hey, Rae," he breathed. "Just getting some work out of the way. What's up?"

The silence at the other end made Carl certain that she somehow knew of his morning spent with TV Land and the Superstation. But he really *had* been working since lunch. He really had.

"Carl, you mind if someone from the office joins us for dinner tonight? He's new, and doesn't know anybody. You mind, sweetie?"

Please, Rae. Not tonight. I'm in no frame of mind.

"I guess that's fine. What time? I'm not cleaned up." Instinctively, Carl combed the fingers of his right hand through his tousled dark hair, as if she could see him in his funk.

"Not until about eight, I think. I should have time to get

home and fix something by then. Okay if I tell him to come by about eight?"

Idol's on at nine. Remind her.

"Sounds like a plan, Rae. Eight." *Damn it, man. Speak!*

"You're so sweet. I know you wanted to see your show. I'll make it up to you, baby."

I sincerely doubt it.

"No problem, Rae. Any friend of yours."

"See you about seven," she said, and hung up. Carl returned the phone to the top of the printer. He tried to re-focus on the spreadsheet before him on the computer monitor. It was no use. Three months on the new job, and already he was sick of tele-commuting. Tired constantly, he had wondered recently wheth-er he was sick, or whether leaving the school world for that of business was indeed killing him. Either way, the last thing in the world he wanted this evening was to host some hotshot broker from Rachel's firm. He'd never leave before Idol, for sure.

Why didn't you just say so?

"What the hell," he muttered. "It's just a couple of hours. Out of a lifetime."

Carl wandered into the kitchen. He poured himself a glass of warm flat Coke from a two-liter container on the island. He downed the soda in several swallows, rubbing his left thumb absently against an orange juice stain on the counter. He walked into the living room, where the television was still on from his lunch date with Matlock five hours ago. He stretched out on the sofa nearest the television, aware of his lethargy, annoyed by the phone call, and swiftly fell asleep.

A sound, abrupt like a thud or whack, awakened him. He groggily wiped dried drool from the left corner of his mouth, rose slowly, and looked around him. Much of the light had gone from the room and, though the vertical blinds were drawn over the sliding glass door leading to the balcony, he could tell that evening was falling fast. He entered the kitchen and glanced at the range clock. Six-forty-six. *Jesus. Just enough time before Rachel gets—*

The rap at the door was heavy, assertive. Carl vaguely wondered whether a knock was what awoke him in the first place. He bent down in front of the range door and used his reflection to smooth his hair and tuck his wrinkled white button-down into his jeans.

Maybe she's got groceries. Door's not even locked.

Carl cleared his throat and strolled slowly toward the door. The knock came again, almost obnoxious in its insistence.

"Coming," he said, hoping that the knocker, especially if it was Rachel, would detect the disapproval in his tone.

Carl opened the bluish-gray metal door.

Before him stood a well-groomed man of about thirty-five, his sandy-blond hair slicked back in a style which reminded Carl of Gordon Gekko in the movie "Wall Street." The man wore an unnecessary tan trenchcoat, unbuttoned, over a dark-blue pinstriped suit.

"Yes?" Carl asked, a bit uncomfortable with the man's casual stance—hands in pockets, slouching to the right, eyes on Carl's.

"I believe I'm early. You mind?"

"Oh. You must be Rachel's guest."

The man straightened and removed his hands from his pockets.

"I suppose I am. May I come in, or shall we plan to dine in the hallway?"

"Um, sure. Please come in."

Carl stepped aside, and the guest strode confidently past him, removing his trenchcoat as he walked. He was several inches over six feet, like Carl, but considerably less filled-out. Lithe, like a tennis player. Carl guessed that they were about the same age, but this fellow was dramatically more fit. Five years earlier, Carl reflected, and that certainly would not have been true. He'd become sedentary since he and Rachel had gotten married two years ago, but he had resolved just a couple of weeks ago to begin working out again. Soon.

The guest held the trenchcoat out toward Carl as if expecting Carl to put it away. Carl, irritated by the suggestion of superiority, made a suggestion of his own.

"Oh, just throw it anywhere. We haven't fixed the place up much yet. Any old chair will do."

"Okidoke," the man replied, and dumped the coat on the dining table.

You know, we might be using that for dinner.

The guest stuck out his hand, smiling smugly. "Your wife didn't give me your name."

"She didn't? Oh. It's—it's Carl." Carl shook the man's hand, and was immediately turned off by the guest's dead-fish handshake, the kind that sometimes made Carl think a man might be a tad light in the loafer. But something about this man seemed as straight as James Bond.

Insincere. That's what that handshake says.

"Hi, Carl. Can a man buy a drink around here?" The man stepped into the living room and sank into Carl's red leather chair.

"I didn't catch your name," Carl offered. *You're over an hour early.* Carl forced a smile. *And you know damn well a red leather chair is never for a guest. Never.*

The guest shifted comfortably in the chair, and placed his wingtipped feet on the red leather ottoman, crossing the left wingtip over the right.

"Smith," he said, examining his fingernails.

Oh, come on.

"I see. What—what's your first name?"

The seated man responded with an incisive look in Carl's

direction, followed by a return to scrutinizing his fingernails.

"John." He smiled and looked back up at Carl. "John will have a screwdriver, Carl."

She'll be home any minute.

"A screwdriver. You got it. John."

Carl turned to go into the kitchen, but the guest's voice stopped him.

"Stoly, Carl, if you don't mind."

"We don't have Stoly. We have Smirnoff." Carl tried to make the words sound informative, but was irritated to hear them emerge defensive. He stood waiting for the guest's response, and got it.

"Okay, big spender."

That did it. Carl crossed to the sofa between the guest and the front hall, and sat heavily. He tried to stare at the man called John, but looked away when the guest regarded him with an amused look.

"Look, John," Carl said quietly, looking at the mauve carpet. "I don't know you. But. This is my apartment. You're sitting in my chair. You're over an hour early for dinner. You're my wife's guest, not mine. So please, I don't know where you come off being so rude, but I ask you, please, don't try my patience."

Carl risked a glance at the guest. The man's eyes clouded briefly, but the quick return of the confident expression forced Carl's eyes back to the floor.

"This is your landlord's apartment, Carl. He's just letting you pay to borrow it for awhile. By the way, were you going to make yourself presentable for dinner? You unemployed or something? Need a couple of bucks?"

Did he hear a word I said? How could Rachel invite a man like this to our new home?

"I—I guess I want to know why you're so early."

The guest reversed wingtips on the ottoman.

"Carl, I'm a successful stockbroker. I know how to pick them. The winners and the losers. I believe in being direct, and I believe that some people have got it and some people haven't." He re-examined his fingernails. "You most assuredly haven't got it, Carl."

Carl had had two bosses speak to him this way in the two years since he'd left the teaching profession in search of more money. He'd allowed them both to get away with it. Not this time.

"Get out of my house," he whispered, staring at a single fuzzy strand of carpet next to his bare right foot.

"I thought you wanted to know why I'm early, Carl."

The strand appeared to be moving, ever so slightly.

"No. I want you to leave."

"I'm early because I wanted you to know that I plan to acquire your wife."

"You plan to—"

"Certainly. You see, Carl, I know how to pick them. She's a winner. You're not. Simple math. It's not adding up to two, big fellow."

"Get out of my home, before I—before I—"

The guest laughed heartily.

"Before you throw a box of Frosted Flakes at me? Get real, Carl. You're nothing. At least, that's what your wife says. Man, you should hear her talk about it. About how much it sucks to be out there involved with life while you watch 'I Dream of Jeannie' and 'Matlock' and feel up your computer every day. And so soon after you've moved into this drab little apartment."

Carl leaped to his feet. "I have a *job!* An important job!"

The guest remained comfortable in the red leather chair.

"Sit down, Carl."

Carl wavered, caught—as he so often was these days—between what he wanted to do and what he would do. He returned to his seat.

"Carl, you've been married what, two years? Your wife tells me you're lousy in bed, have no ambition, and she married you because she thought she'd never meet a man like me. Biological clock and all that crap. Most women I've known are in the same boat as your wife, except they married to gain access to resources, big fellow. Resources for them and their kids. So they stay with their husbands, and play happy house for their friends and their alumni magazines. But not *your* wife. She didn't marry you for resources, Carl. So you're smack out of luck. You don't have access to offer your wife, Carl. Or ambition. Or energy. Or passion. So, you can give her to me."

Carl summoned the courage he thought he needed to defend himself.

"If I had a gun, I swear I'd kill you," he breathed.

"If you had a gun, I swear you'd stick the barrel in your mouth."

An ache spread in Carl's throat, and he fought the tears that would embarrass him in front of this monster.

"Rachel would never say those things," he rasped. "Never."

"She would, and she did. Just this morning, as a matter of fact. How about that fancy screwdriver, big fellow?"

"She'll—she'll be here any minute now. We'll ask her. She knows my new job has possibilities. And I don't watch television all day. And we, we love each other. A lot. So you're not so smart. If—if you don't leave now, I'll have you arrested."

"Mind telling me what law I'm breaking, big fellow?"

Where is she? Why did she let him come here ahead of her? She must've gotten tied down at work. Unless—

The guest rose and crossed the living room to the balcony door. He opened the vertical blinds to reveal the last shades of dusky gray gasping for air as night pressed its weight down upon the day.

"Carl, the reason I'll succeed in acquiring your wife," the

man said as he turned from the glass doors, "is that I am in possession of something that is not exactly one of your, ah, assets."

"Please. I don't want to hear your—"

"Passion, big fellow. That's what she'll see in me that she doesn't see in you. Passion for all that interests me. I don't live my life through a computer screen, Carl. I don't entertain myself or others with a television set. I possess both. They don't possess *me*. And I will possess your wife, because I have the resource to which she wants access. She's better than all the other women I've known, Carl, because the resource she wants from a man is passion..."

The guest took a step toward Carl. "Passion for all that interests me, Carl. I don't hide anything. I think you see that already. And it's why you already know you will lose her to me." The guest's face was inches from Carl's. "Now get me that screwdriver before I passionately beat you to a pathetic pulp."

Carl, tears streaming down his cheeks, the churns of self-pity alive in his gut, turned and retreated toward the kitchen. She would be here soon.

As he opened the cabinet which housed the liquor, he looked out toward the living room. His eye was drawn by movement, past the furniture, past the visitor who rocked cockily on his feet with his hands in his pockets.

The movement was, from this distance, a mangle of colors that changed every second or two, seemingly for no reason at all. As his right hand closed on the bottle of vodka, his wet eyes focused more clearly on the constantly shifting images coming from the far corner of the living room. The more the images shifted, the more the churning in Carl's gut turned to rage.

He had never turned off the television set.

Suddenly the ludicrousness of his life pointed a forefinger at him. It poked him in the chest, like a bully in a schoolyard.

Carl set his jaw. He examined the bottle in his hand. The rage climbed out of his gut and into his arms and legs as he rushed madly toward the guest, charged past him, surprised him with his decisiveness, and smashed the vodka bottle into the television screen, obliterating the blather of a news show into countless pieces of dark glass. Turning, he faced John Smith. Drool ran from the left corner of Carl's mouth, but he did not care.

Smith focused on the drool, and put his hands up in self-defense.

Carl advanced toward the guest, the reek of vodka filling the room, his right hand holding high the shattered bottle. He would kill this man, just as he'd killed the television set and the morons who lived in it. He would end this man who had come into his home and been so, so...so

insightful.

Carl stopped. He saw the fear in the man's eyes, but saw something else, something which didn't fit.

It was pleasure. But no longer mocking, or cocky. Just pleased. Frightened and pleased.

"Get out of my home. *Now.* There's no supper for you here."

The guest wasted no time in retrieving his trenchcoat from the dining table. As he put the coat on and advanced toward the front door, the guest turned and faced Carl.

"I'll find my supper somewhere else, big fellow."

And the guest exited quietly.

Carl, exhilarated and strangely clear-headed, returned to the kitchen and carefully laid the bottle remnant on the counter next to the microwave. His heart raced as he returned to the living room and sat confidently in his red leather chair. As he cooled off in the silence, he remembered, fondly, the first months with Rachel, nearly three years ago. The year before the wedding. The year before the career change. The constant, gorgeous music. The slow dances before bed. Touch football Sunday mornings in the park with strangers and friends alike. Weekend drives to the beach, where they played putt-putt at low tide, digging holes with their hands for a nine-hole course.

They had passed books between each other. Classics, thrillers, spy novels, short stories, poetry...and always the music. They had made love to Santana's "Europa," and Stan Getz's "Keep Me in Your Heart," seldom forgetting Pat Metheny's "The Truth Will Always Be." Each time was exquisitely unlike any other as they celebrated the passing of a day that had never happened before, and the coming of one the world had never seen.

Carl wondered where it had gone. He didn't think, now, sitting here amid the piercing scent of vodka, that any of it had ever gotten old. That first year together, he'd leapt out of bed each morning, the spring staying in his step all day as he taught his classes with a verve which enlivened even the most reticent students. As he remembered, he thought back to when he had taught Richter's *The Light in the Forest*. Strange that only now did he recall the line from the slave character, Bejance, about any man being a slave if he pulls burdens which mean nothing to the soul inside of him.

And he had missed her each day in the best of ways — the kind that says *I get to see her again.*

He rose from the red leather chair and sank back into the sofa nearest the deceased television set. She liked to sit here. To read here. She still did, while he sat toadlike in front of his computer terminal down the hall in the den, visiting inane websites and other substitutes for real living.

When did it begin?

He pressed his face against the back cushion, trying to catch her scent, but the vodka's smell was more powerful and more... recent. He tried and tried and tried, deep heaving sniffs of air against the cushion, but he just couldn't quite catch it. Not right here. But he would.

If I haven't lost her.

A sound, abrupt like a thud or whack, awakened him. He groggily wiped dried drool from the left corner of his mouth, rose slowly, and looked around him. Much of the light had gone from the room and, though the vertical blinds were drawn over the sliding glass door leading to the balcony, he could tell that evening was falling fast. He entered the kitchen and glanced at the range clock. Six-forty-six. *Jesus. Just enough time before—*

Wait a minute.

He could smell her. She was at the door. He was sure of it. Thrilled, he hurried into the living room and turned off the television set, glancing with disdain as he did so at the two nitwits pontificating on some useless idiotic subject that had nothing whatever to do with him.

He ran to the front door and flung it open.

And there she stood, groceries in both arms. *What a beautiful woman she is.*

"What a beautiful woman you are," he blurted, and took the groceries from his puzzled wife, who followed him into the kitchen.

"Sweetie?" she said as he set the bags down and kissed her. "Are you all right?"

"Of course I'm all right. I'll pick the music tonight, if you don't mind."

"The music? Why, that's—that's fine. But I thought you wanted to watch Idol. It's Wednesday. You don't like to miss the elimination show."

"Not me. I'll go take a quick shower. Join me?"

She looked around her as if she expected someone to jump out and end the joke.

"Really?" she said, a smile growing.

"Really. In case your friend is early."

She slapped her right palm against her forehead, as if she'd forgotten something.

"Oh, my God, Carl, I'm so sorry. I forgot to call you."

"What? What is it, Rae?"

"Frank got called away by a client about an hour ago." She took a playful step forward and began unbuttoning Carl's shirt.

"Is that so?" Carl asked as he cupped her hands lightly while they did their deft work.

"That's so, big fellow," she said, kissing his chest as she pulled the shirt away. "He asked for a raincheck. Said he'll find his supper somewhere else."

Carl laughed softly at the man's obvious inability to separate the good things in life from the mundane. He scooped his wife into the air and down the hall, wondering on the way whether perhaps they shouldn't step out to Jordy's later for Stoly screwdrivers and some swing.

THE FIRST KEY

They say there's a good way and a bad way to learn a lesson. I guess I learned mine the good way, but I was lucky. Damn lucky, you ask me. So pay attention.

I was only three days on the job, you see, and already I was late for an appointment. Hell, I was young in those days, but like I told you already, that's no excuse. The alarm buzzed at six, but I smacked the snooze button nine times after. *Nine times,* like I had all day. My dad would've called me a lazy nimrod. That's what he always called me when I slept in on Saturdays. Anyways, by the time I got out of bed it was seven-thirty, and I was supposed to be at this municipal government office by eight. God knows I still hate even thinking about it. I raced through the shower, all kinds of mess going through my mind. Second chances, wasted opportunities, shirked responsibilities. Unemployment. Death, of course. But that goes without saying.

My shaving hand was shaking, out of control. I could practically see the boss in the mirror. Mr. Bucci had spent a whole entire day training me on the "Five Keys to the Door of Success." The first key, he said, and the most important key, was Punctuality. "Sal," he said, "how can a man finish first if he always shows up last?" Then he looked at me for about ten seconds. I could see it meant a lot to him, being on time and all, so I wrote it down in my new daytimer. But I have to admit, I was young, like you, and I wrote it down mainly so he'd think I was paying real close attention.

Punctuality. I was at Clausen for what, six years? Six years, and nobody ever said anything about Punctuality being the first key to some Door of Success. They didn't teach us squat about business ethics, you see. Too busy telling us what to do.

But you should've seen me shaving. Miracle I didn't cut myself to hell. So anyways, here I was about to disappoint my new boss on my very first appointment. Mr. Bucci had even gone to the trouble of setting up the appointment, and was going as far as making the introductions for me. But he was real clear with his last words, the night before on the phone. "Eight sharp. Remember the First Key."

Christ, I could throw up even now, just thinking about it.

So there I was, pulling into the office parking lot at eight-fifteen in my old broken-down seventy-five Volvo, the one my big brother the banker had until the heart attack. I could feel my heartbeat thumping everywhere. I mean *everywhere*. Temples, ears, cheeks, especially my gut. It was a good thing my stomach was empty, or I'd have launched for sure.

What the hell are you looking at? There's nothing out there but concrete, boy. I told you to pay attention.

So I'm walking across the parking lot, thinking to myself, "What if this guy's a hardliner, a stickler for punctuality, this guy from Municipal Projects?" It was messing with my coordination, thinking about being dumped by Mr. Bucci on my third day, and I almost tripped when I missed the rhythm of that big revolving door going into the office building.

You follow what I'm saying, don't you? This guy from Municipal Projects? If his Five Keys are the same as Mr. Bucci's, I'm a dead man.

When you were a kid, and the teacher made you get up and make a presentation or a speech to the whole class, do you remember how hard it was to breathe? You figure everybody can see your paper shaking, watch your heartbeat on your face?

Well, that's what I was like when I reached the elevator. For good measure, it was the kind of elevator I've always hated — the glass kind, with the curved glass walls so everybody yakking in the lobby can watch you on your way to screwing up your future. Or coming back down without one.

I pressed the 'Up' arrow. Big, round button, and I almost missed it, my finger's shaking so bad. *Look* at me when I'm talking to you. I'm explaining what you're doing here. God *damn*.

So then I'm thinking, I'm thinking, I'm *thinking*, what are the other Keys to the Door of Success? The Man had just taught them to me, for Christ sake. Even gave me a memo sheet with bullet points. The works. And I remember one of them, like God put it there for me to remember.

Hope.

Maybe he's still there, this guy from Municipal Projects. Maybe. Oh, God, please let there be a maybe.

Yeah, I thought. And "maybe" he'll say, "Okay, Bucci, I gave you your chance to make a competitive bid. Didn't have all day to wait on you and your boy."

I kind of mumbled that last part out loud, so I was real embarrassed when I discovered that I wasn't alone waiting for the elevator. This older fellow, about sixty or so, dressed like a college professor, old-fashioned bifocals, tweed jacket, is standing there right next to me, reading the sports section. I can still see the damn thing, folded in half, a USA Today sports page. Funny how things stick in your mind. I remember thinking how wonderful it would be if I were actually five minutes *early* and had the luxury of studying last night's Cubs boxscore on a leisurely ride up the elevator.

I wanted to trade places with this old man real bad. *Real* bad. He looked so damn comfortable, like he'd just finished his eggs and coffee and was going back to his office to stretch out nice and easy before the masseuse arrived.

Then the elevator bell tinkled—dinged—whatever you call it, and the glass door was in front of us. This fat middle-aged lady in a mink coat and hat comes out, no doubt on her way to a pleasant day uncomplicated by the Five Keys to the Door of Success. This old tweed guy says "After you," really pleasant. He kind of waves me in with the sports section. So I enter and press the fourteenth floor. The old man comes in and says, "Fourteen, if you don't mind."

At first I don't realize that the man is speaking to me. The door swishes shut, and I turn around and see that we're the only two people in the elevator.

"Pardon?" I whisper. I'd meant to use my vocal chords, but they failed me. I was that scared about the First Key, you see.

The guy looks up casually from his paper. "If you could hit fourteen I would—oh, it's already lit up. Sorry."

I cleared my throat. "That's okay," I said. It felt good to speak, sort of like talking to a priest before your execution. It may not change anything, but it feels better than the facts. I decided to relieve some of my anxiety by speaking again.

"You work in this building here, sir?" I was such a moron. What difference did it make? Still, I breathed more easily.

"Just until tomorrow, yes. I'm retiring, and I'm delighted to say it."

"I see." *Go ahead,* I think to myself. *Blow some steam.*

"Retiring from what, if you don't mind my inquiring?" I said "inquiring" because it was polite vocabulary. Mr. Bucci had made a special point of teaching me that the right vocabulary assists the good businessman in getting the customer's guard down. It isn't one of the Five Keys, but it certainly helps turn the knob.

The old guy looks at me and smiles. "I work in Municipal Projects. Fancy name for 'Stuff the City Does to Waste Tax Dollars'." He chuckles sort of self-deprecatingly.

Well, I've got to tell you. What a small world, I thought. You see, Mr. Bucci and I were going to the same department. Municipal Projects. Nineteen floors in this building, and this fellow and I are headed for the same place. What were the odds? So I say—

Okay. Nineteen to one, I guess. Wise guy. Or maybe eighteen-to-one if they got no thirteenth floor, and I really don't remember and we're getting off track. So shut up and let me finish. The point is we're going to the same department.

"No kidding!" I say. "That's where *I'm* headed!"

The fellow smiles again, but like he's tired or something. But he's nice. Very nice. Says, "Isn't that something. Small building, eh? Who are you going to see?"

"The head of purchasing and estimating. Guy named Telder."

The fellow frowns for a second, then goes back to smiling.

"You must work for Paul Bucci. I'm, I'm Frank Telder. I must confess I'm relieved that we're both late. Was having breakfast across the street and lost all track of the time." He shakes his head like he thinks he's an idiot or something. "Sometimes I get going on the sports page and—poof!—there goes the time and I'm late."

Now, this guy looks like he hasn't made a mistake since he was in grammar school, yet here he's done the same stupid thing I have. We're both late, though Mr. Bucci's only going to be miffed at me, as you of all people can imagine. So, I smile back at him and say, "I'm as relieved as you are, Mr. Telder. I just started working for Mr. Bucci, and I overslept. On the third day of a new job. Can you beat that for being a schmuck?"

The old man just laughs and adjusts the lapels of his tweed jacket, and the elevator stops and dings. I shouldn't be feeling better, just from a thirty-second conversation, but I am.

"Here's fourteen," the guy says, and he waves me through the door. I stop and stand on the gray carpet in the hallway, looking in both directions for Mr. Bucci.

The old guy walks on down the hallway on the left, and— *Listen*, if there's something interesting out there, I wish you'd share it with me...

I didn't think so.

So the guy from Municipal Projects walks on down the hallway on the left. He turns and says, "Are you coming?" He holds out the newspaper like he wants to wave me ahead. I think to myself, "He doesn't seem very worried." I figured that was because he was on his own turf and all.

"Actually, I'm supposed to meet my boss here in the hall," I say, and it's true, and I'm shitting bricks, because I know how miffed the Man is by now. Probably he'd been standing there outside the elevator, looking like a jerk, for fifteen minutes waiting for my sorry rear end. Went looking for me, most likely, or was calling my apartment.

The man from Municipal Projects jingled some keys in his right pocket.

"Well, do me a favor before you come in, okay?" he says.

"Sure," I say, though naturally I don't really mean it at this point.

"Tell Paul that I really don't want to hear any new numbers today. The bids are sealed, and I'd like just once to do this right. Retire with my head held high. He should be able to understand that. Don't you think?"

I think to myself, "Whatever." But I remember what Mr. Bucci said in that first training session. Never let a customer know what you're *really* thinking. Unless you're discontinuing the business relationship, that is, and that should *only* be when the relationship is no longer profitable. The true one-minute manager knows how to stroke. The hell with sincerity. The Man always said there's only one synonym for ethics: The Bottom Line. That's the only ethic in business, and the only reason for learning the Five Keys.

So I say, "My pleasure." And I smile real big so he knows I mean it.

He raises his sports page to me and says, "Thank you," and continues on his way.

I take the smile off, and my heart starts pounding, because I'm so late and Mr. Bucci has left. At least that's what I thought. But then the elevator dings behind me, and I turn around in time to see the door slide open. And there he is.

And he's miffed. Christ, he's ticked. Asks me a rhetorical question about why the hell I think he took the time to teach me the Five Keys to the Door of Success. He doesn't let me answer, just waves his hand like I'm a nuisance, and I guess I was, violating the First Key and all.

But like I said, I was lucky. Luckier than you, anyway. We walk on down to Municipal Projects, and Mr. Bucci tells the secretary we're here to see Mr. Telder. Telder comes out of his office and says, "Come in, gentlemen," and tells his secretary to take a coffee break. We follow Telder into his office, Mr. Bucci first, then me. Telder closes the door, and the whole atmosphere changes.

"Listen, Paul," Telder says, standing in the middle of the room. I guess not offering us a seat was his way of saying it would be a short meeting. "I'm not buying today. I thought that was clear on the phone. I want to retire on a clear conscience."

Mr. Bucci just folds his arms, cool as an October breeze. Doesn't say a word. Sure enough, the customer fills the silence, just like always.

"What I mean is, Paul, I can't give you the contract on my last day." And Telder folds his arms too. Battle of the folding arms. Two old veterans.

Well, I knew it was over when Mr. Bucci smiled and stuck out his hand. Telder shook it, and seemed truly relieved that there would be no argument or haggling on his last day. And I was relieved as well, because it meant I'd finally get to do my job, and because it meant my being late hadn't cost Mr. Bucci this opportunity to discontinue a business relationship.

Mr. Bucci says, "Frank, I don't know about your conscience, but I would indeed feel terrible if this wasn't your last day." And he looks at me. And that's it.

I pull out my .44 and whip Telder backhand across the face. I guess his face is old, because his left cheek flaps apart like a peeled banana. He flops down on the floor, tries to fold up like a ball. But Mr. Bucci had said before that the guy from Municipal Projects needed a lesson in business ethics, and he wanted the lesson taken like a man.

So while I pull Telder up, him bleeding and spitting and wheezing, Mr. Bucci gives him the lesson. I still remember every word, all these years later. He started right after I brought a knee to Municipal's middle.

"You see, Frank, a business relationship is based upon features and benefits," the boss says, and begins to pace like a professor in front of a class. "The feature is just a description. The benefit is the *explanation* of what's *good* about the feature. A feature without a benefit is like food taken intravenously. You don't know it's good until you *taste* it." He pauses as I break Municipal's teeth with my elbow. I probably shouldn't have done the teeth like that, because the old man's gurgling forces Mr. Bucci to speak louder. But Mr. Bucci adapts and continues the lesson.

"In our bid, the feature was filled potholes. The benefit was five grand in your pocket. But Frank, on this day you ignored the Fifth Key to the Door of Success. Consistency. How many deals have we made over the years? And now, you choose to become inconsistent, violate the Fifth Key. That's bad ethics, Frank. Inconsistency is hell on a bottom line, my friend."

I think Mr. Bucci allowed himself a sigh when Telder spit

out some teeth and tried to mumble something about the Right Thing.

"Frank, Frank, Frank..." the boss says, shaking his head and standing over the defeated bureaucrat. "Let's look at the Five Keys, shall we? And then you tell me about ethics. First, we have Punctuality, my friend. Did I violate this ethic, this key to good business, this first factor in making the sale? No. You did. Today and many other days. So did my new subordinate, who will be lucky if the bottom line allows him no, ah, reprimand." Of course, I look away when the boss says this, but I think he was looking a hole right through me. As a matter of fact, I think he was really talking to *me* the whole time. It was *my* business ethics he was talking about. Telder was just a prop for the lesson.

"Second, Frank, we have Anticipation. The good salesman *anticipates* the customer's objections. I anticipated yours today. Did you anticipate mine? I think not. Again, on your last day, you flatulate in the direction of the Five Keys." The boss reaches down and pulls Municipal's head up by the hair.

"The Third Key, Frank, is Perseverence. When you said yesterday on the phone that you were retiring and hence would award this contract to another of the sealed bids, did I accept your lame excuse and go meekly on my way? No. I insisted upon this appointment, until you agreed to host Sal and me so graciously and, I must say now, quietly. The man who observes and respects the Five Keys is standing, while he who spits on them now spits teeth."

The boss drops the head like a bowling ball.

"The Fourth Key, Frank, is Thoroughness. The old follow-through. We could leave you here to think about the Five Keys, but that would not be thorough. Once a man has lost his ethics, he is not to be trusted. Sal, please be thorough."

I step forward and put two bullets in Municipal's brain. Mr.

Bucci leads me out to the secretary's office, and we sit while he talks about the close relationship between the fourth and fifth keys, Thoroughness and Consistency. After ten minutes, he suggests that perhaps there should be six keys to the Door of Success. I ask him what that should be, and he looks at his watch, smiles, and says "Patience."

The door from the hall opens and in comes Municipal's secretary. She's got a green coffee mug in her hand. I can still see the thing.

The boss says to her, very politely, "Excuse me, but do you know who I am?"

She studies him for a second, then looks at me.

"Why, yes, Mr. Bucci. But I don't know your friend."

The boss stands. "Did old Frank let you know I was coming this morning, by chance?"

"Oh, no, Mr. Bucci. He prefers that your meetings are kept confidential."

"How anticipative of him. Sal, please make sure today's meeting is kept, ah, confidential."

So I get up and remember the fourth key. Two in the brain.

Thoroughness, my friend. One of the Five Keys, never to forget.

I asked Mr. Bucci if it was okay if I grabbed the sports page from Telder's office, and then I went in, found it folded on the desk with a smidgeon of blood on it, wiped it against Municipal's pants, and we left. All the way down in the elevator, I could see Mr. Bucci was still miffed, but it was okay. The Bottom Line, my friend. The ultimate ethic.

I got to tell you, though. It feels *good* when you think you've screwed up, you're late, missing the First Key, your life's about over and then, *voila*, everything's fine.

So maybe it was a miracle. I don't know. But I learned my lesson, the good way, and I was lucky.

Anyways, I tell you all this because the *best* way to learn a lesson is to listen to people who know what the hell they're talking about. The ones that have been there. You didn't listen very well, and you weren't lucky enough to fill up the bottom line.

Pop quiz. I lied about one of the Five Keys. If you can tell me which one was a lie, this won't be your last day. I'll give you ten seconds...

Well, I'll be damned. You were paying attention after all. Hope. You're right, of course. Hope is not one of the Five Keys to the Door of Success.

Funny you got that one right. Okay, you're luckier than I thought. Let's go get a beer, and I'll show you how the Man liked it done. Fix your bottom line. God rest the old man's soul.

CARPOOL

C harley Tolliver stepped past the dog bowls and into the middle of the kitchen. He scraped the flat of his black wingtip sole against the Spanish tile, back and forth, breaking the silence with the sound of sandy gristle. It was seven o'clock now. Nobody was home.

He opened the pantry door. Right, he thought. They're all hiding in here amongst the Chef Boyardee and the Del Monte and the high-fiber oatmeal packets.

Charley closed the pantry door and stood still again. If he strained hard enough, he might hear something, he thought. After ten seconds it occurred to him that the ringing in his right ear must be there all the time.

Where the hell were the dogs? Two Labrador retrievers don't ignore the presence of their master, or of each other, long enough to let a ringing go off in a man's ear for long. Especially not Sheff and Buster. Hell, the ringing probably came from those two knuckleheads in the first place. Normally the mere creak of the pantry door would have brought them barking and sprinting from the nether regions of the house, because the dog chow resided in the pantry.

Nobody was home. For God's sake, he thought.

Charley walked through the house one more time, his wingtips clomping loud on each of the sixteen wooden stairs. He entered the children's bedroom. The top and bottom bunks were made, the Winnie the Pooh and Tigger bedspreads perfectly aligned with the white side paneling of the bunk structure. *Naturally*, he thought. Julia wouldn't want to leave the house a mess instead of taking the time to call her husband at any of his *three* contact numbers to tell him that she's packing up the kids and the dogs and the hamsters and the fish and the bunny and there's Chef Boyardee in the kitchen so have a nice life, Charley.

He picked up a Leapster that had a game cartridge sticking out of the top. This one was Ashley's. Ashley would rather dive head-first into hot volcanic lava than go anywhere without her Leapster, Charley knew. He was comforted by the presence of the Leapster, and then even more so by the discovery of Kelly's Leapster next to a stuffed Eeyore on the girls' shared desk. Either Julia had not thought of the Leapsters in her rush to get the kids and the dogs and the fish and the hamsters and the bunny out of the house after making the bunk beds and not calling her husband with the news, or they weren't *really* gone. Maybe the dogs had to go to the vet for an emergency visit, and they'd all be traipsing back into the house with hot fried chicken from the drive-thru any second now. Maybe the dogs had an emergency. Sure! She didn't have *time* to call, because the dogs had an emergency.

Sure. And so did the fish and the hamsters and the bunny. Of course. Sure. And the feeling returned that he had been left alone, like a child counting to a hundred in a hide-and-seek game while the other kids are running away to watch TV and laugh at the sucker they left at the big oak tree.

Even Julia wouldn't do that, he thought. But the minivan was gone. No note. Just two Leapsters in the girls' room to say Julia wasn't perfect.

Charley walked swiftly through the master bedroom. Odd that the bed wasn't made, but he didn't have time for that right now, and he hurried back downstairs. Who could spend time looking at their own bed when their family was missing? Charley knew that he was a much better man than that, and checked the pantry one more time, peeking behind the hot water heater, before slamming the pantry door in agitation and heading for the TV room to—

He stopped in the marble foyer. The sound had come from the front door, as if beckoning him to check outside. But it was dusk now, the late September sun running away from the night. He did not want to check outside. After all, he had *begun* outside, hadn't he? He had pulled the Land Rover into the driveway at six-fifteen and the minivan wasn't there. What else was there to check outside, for Christ's sake?

He took another step toward the TV room and the doorbell rang. Charley froze. God, they could *see* him from out there, those stupid little useless windows framing the front door at night just so they can see in when you can't see out and God, oh God, what if it's the police and something's happened to Julia and the kids? The dogs too? And the fish and the hamsters and the...

It would not be the police. *Open the door*, a voice told him.

"I can't," he whispered. "I can't."

He left the foyer and continued on to the TV room, ignoring the ringing doorbell as someone obnoxiously kept pushing the damned thing and *please won't you just stop it I'm looking for my goddamned family won't you just give me a break?? Sell it somewhere else.*

Julia had left the TV on. She's definitely losing her touch, Charley thought. The volume was up, too. Funny, he thought, but the ringing in his right ear hadn't picked this up when he was in the kitchen. He glanced at the television screen in time to see a bathrobed man who had guest-starred on a million TV shows open the front door of his house and welcome a visitor. Charley recognized the disheveled, trenchcoat-clad visitor as Columbo from the old detective series he watched when he was a kid. But that did not matter now, not when he was searching for his family.

There were no Leapsters in the TV room, so Charley went back out to the foyer. He was relieved that the obnoxious doorbell ringer had given up and left, because he really needed to find Julia and the kids. It was time to check with the neighbors, just to see if anything suspicious had happened, maybe while they had been mowing their lawns or tending to their gardens.

He turned on the front porch light and peered outside through the stupid windows. He mused that they weren't so stupid when the front porch light was on.

There was nobody outside, at least not for as far as the porch light would illuminate. He considered removing his suit coat before going next door to the Hinmans', because they were casual people who couldn't wait to get out of their work clothes every day. Charley had never understood why Mark and Sarah Hinman always walked around the neighborhood barefoot at their age, but they did. Weird stuff, the Hinmans, but Julia liked them and was always going to their house to have a glass of wine when Charley was still at work and the kids were at soccer practice on somebody else's carpool day.

He decided to leave the suit coat on. If he had learned one thing in his years at the bank, it was that there was no such thing as being overdressed. Mark and Sarah Hinman had every right to do as they wanted in a free country, but the sensible thing to do when you were market vice president was to err on the side of being overdressed. He straightened his paisley tie, the one Julia was always calling a relic of the eighties, and ventured out onto the porch and down the steps to the brick walk.

Two spotlights switched on as the motion detectors did their jobs and Charley could see to cross through an opening between the Leland cypresses dividing the Tolliver and Hinman properties.

He rang the doorbell, re-straightening his tie. Julia wouldn't go anywhere without the Hinmans knowing about it. Especially not with the kids, the dogs, the hamsters, the bunny and the fish. Maybe she was even here right now. Except for the minivan, of course. The damned minivan.

Charley heard what sounded like mild argument from inside. Muffled, like angry whispers. They know something, he thought. They *know* where they've gone. And not even the consideration of a phone call, knowing that I'm pulling my hair out with worry over there…Talk about taking sides. Neighbors should choose neutrality, for God's—

The door opened. Mark Hinman stood there with a Heineken in his right hand and gave Charley the same goofy grin he always did.

Charley wasn't buying it.

"Evening, Mark," Charley offered.

"Why, Charley! What a pleasant surprise. Sarah! It's Charley Tolliver! Come in, Charley. Please come in. Can I get you a beer? Glass of chardonnay? I know you go back and forth."

Charley marched past Hinman and into the dimly-lit living room. He looked left and right and turned back to face Hinman.

"*I* go back and forth, Hinman? *I* go back and forth? You and your wife have been keeping secrets with Julia for months. *Months!* And now she's missing. Julia and the kids and the dogs and—"

"My God, man!" exclaimed Hinman, setting his Heineken down on the living room coffee table. "Missing? How do you mean? Sarah! Come quick!"

A door opened down the hall, and Sarah Hinman entered the room in bare feet and an oversized white tee-shirt that made her look like she wasn't wearing anything on the bottom.

"Charley! What a pleasant surprise! How's—"

"I'm not here to play nice, Sarah. You can stop pretending

that you didn't expect to hear from me tonight. Julia and the girls aren't home. I was just wondering...if you saw anything strange today."

"Well, Charley," Sarah said, her face registering what Charley thought was a creditable attempt at surprise. "Maybe they went to soccer practice?" Nice, the way she said it as a question. Charley was disgusted at such pretense. He had never cared for it, socially or otherwise.

"They *did* go to soccer practice, Sarah. She had the carpool today, so I guess she didn't manage to be here downing shots with you and Mark and God knows who else you conveniently invite to your little shindigs. But she should've been home by six. I came home to an empty house, and, and—"

"Charley, why don't you sit down," Sarah said. "Can we get you a beer? Or..."

There it was. She shot a look at Hinman there. The briefest of quick, just the dartiest of a flick, but she sure did, Charley knew. They *know.*

"Look," Charley said, hands in pockets, trying to look calm. "They're not home. The *dogs* aren't home. She even took the aquarium. The bunny. The bunny's cage. Seven *hamsters,* for Christ's sake. She's left me, and I think you know why. So yes, Sarah, I accept your gracious offer. Beer sounds good."

Sarah Hinman nodded and left the room. The ensuing silence was awkward, as Charley risked a glance at Hinman.

"Where are they, Mark?" Charley asked. "I know you know."

Hinman shifted uneasily, taking a long look in the direction of the kitchen.

"Charley, I don't know what you think I know. We only had the occasional drink with your wife. Only when the kids had soccer practice. That's all, Charley. I'm sorry they're not there. I really am. But I'm going to say one thing without Sarah in the room. I'm sorry about Julia and the kids not being home, but it *really* gets to my wife when you talk about us as if we're lushes. You've talked that way about us for months, to anyone who will listen. You think it doesn't get back to us?"

Silence hovered expectantly. Charley mulled a response, but decided to take the high road and say nothing. Hinman was in denial was all.

"We're *not* lushes, Charley. A couple of drinks a night. We're not the reason your family's not at home, Charley. I think you know that. You've known that for a long time. Maybe if you— oh, here's Sarah with that beer for you, Charley."

Hinman stepped back, as if Sarah really needed five feet of space to give her neighbor a cold beer. They were acting strangely indeed, Charley thought. He accepted the Heineken and found a seat on the tan leather sofa facing the Hinmans' stacked-stone fireplace.

"Mind if I sit down?"

"Not at all," said Hinman.

The Hinmans did not sit down. They were hiding something, and Charley was going to get to the bottom of it, no matter how rude they could get with a couple of rounds in them.

"Look. I'm only asking you to help me here. They've gone somewhere. Julia didn't even leave a note. No phone call. Not even an email, for God's sake. A text message. *Nothing.* And I think it has something to do with her little visits here. I can't tell you the times I've come home, and the minivan is right there in the driveway, the kids are at soccer practice, and is my wife home doing anything productive? No. Of course not. She's over here. You don't want me to call you lushes, Hinman. That's fine. But you turned my *wife* into a lush, and God knows what else. And now she's packed up the kids, the dogs, the bunny, the hamsters, even the goddamned *fish,* and not even the courtesy of a simple note. Even just 'Have a nice life, Charley. You can keep the dog bowls.' *Nothing.*"

"Charley, if you'd just listen to reason, maybe we could help you figure this out," Hinman said, but Charley knew he didn't mean it. They had certainly been Julia's closest counsel, meddling in another family's business when *nothing* was their business on their side of those goddamned Leland cypresses.

"The way you helped Julia figure it out?" Charley spit the words out and took a long swig from the green bottle.

"That's uncalled for and you know it." Hinman took a step toward the front door. "I'm a patient man, but I have my limits. Get out of my house."

"Mark!" Sarah Hinman gasped. "Please!"

"No, Sarah, there will be no more pleases. No more 'Try to understand where Charley's coming from' and 'Try to understand how people cope' and all that crap. *Charley* needs to understand where he's coming from. Don't you, Charley. And then go in another direction. Here's some free advice for you, jackass. Be the—"

"*Mark! Please!*" Sarah turned and ran from the room. Her oversized tee shirt hunched upward as she went. Charley noticed that she was indeed wearing something on her bottom, and was relieved that she wore something on her bottom at this hour. What with Julia being here about now on so many evenings.

Hinman pursued his point, moving closer toward the front door.

"You see what you're doing to my wife? Do you, Charley? Before I hit you in the ass with this door, I'm going to give you that free advice. Won't even charge you interest. That's a term you understand in your profession, isn't it? Be the banker, Charley. Be the banker. Do the calculation. Check the repayment schedule, jackass."

Charley tried to swallow the lump in his throat. The man's staggering insensitivity was…was…He could not cry in front of Hinman. Hinman might even tell Julia, and then she'd really have the upper hand. If she wasn't gone forever, of course, and if she didn't take the children to forever with her.

Hinman pressed on. "Whatever the damned hell you people do all day. You say we turned your wife into a lush, Charley? Check your precious compound interest, man. It's being compounded daily. You're the one who's paying it, Charley. Not us. Now get out of my house. *Now.*"

Hinman opened the door and stood aside, waving his left hand toward the gaping darkness.

Charley stood, raising a shaking green bottle to his lips, sipping at the lip of the bottle but getting only loud oxygen, moving toward the rectangular hole, passing through it into the night, hearing the door close but not slam behind him as he stumbled in the direction of the Leland cypresses.

When he reached the front yard, he looked back at the driveway, illuminated by the motion-detection spotlights that dutifully went to work upon his return.

The minivan was not there. Julia had not had a change of heart. No epiphany. No sudden thought that the children loved their daddy, would miss him terribly, awfully, all day at school, pining for their father as their lives were ripped to shreds in a single momentary lapse of judgment by their mother.

Back in the house, he checked the TV room again. It wasn't tuned to Nickelodeon. Boomerang? No. Cartoon Network? Stop it! *Stop it!*

Charley went upstairs and brushed his teeth. He allowed himself one defiance of Julia's rules, and skipped the floss.

He removed his suit jacket and tossed it onto the chaise in the corner. That was two, he thought. If she wanted him to floss and to hang up his clothes and put his socks in the hamper, she would just have to come home and quit this nonsense of being gone. If not for him, then for the kids. Kids needed a daddy to protect them, didn't they? Didn't they?

He stood and looked at the bed. He wondered whether any-body else of his gender had ever been in it. Whether anybody else who had ever been in it might be in the minivan right this minute with Julia and the kids and Sheff and Buster and…

Maybe they arranged to hook up for the trip at pickup time at soccer practice. Leave Somebody Else's car there and just drive off in the minivan and go to California or Canada or the Carolinas or wherever until Julia wakes up one day and says there are flings and there are real things and Julia's real thing and my kids' real thing is a market vice president waiting for Mommy to have the epiphany and bring the minivan home. Please, Mommy. Bring the minivan home.

He climbed into bed and set the alarm for six like he always did. He was about to pull the chain on the light when he re-membered that maybe she called while he was at the Hinmans'.

He got out of bed and went downstairs, half expecting the dogs to follow him in a cacophony of excitement about the prospect of a treat or some leftovers. In the kitchen, he grabbed a pen and the pad of Post-Its, though of course he realized that if Julia left a message he would remember it. But you never knew. You never knew.

The machine reported that there were no new messages and said 'First Saved Message' before Charley hurriedly pressed the Off button.

He re-checked the incoming mail box in the plastic mail sort-er Julia bought and put next to the phone when she was feel-ing particularly anal one day. He had forgotten to bring today's mail in tonight, so all that was in the sorter next to the phone was the power bill and the cards from his dad and mom and his brother and Julia's sister and her God-forsaken mom and dad and all those people from the church, and that big manila envelope from State Farm.

He knew he needed to try to sleep, even though it was only 8:15 and he usually checked the Now Playing list on the DVR right about now. If he went to bed early, he'd get almost ten hours. Enough to go on to forever tomorrow, contact the authorities, drive around, everything, because after all, he had rights. He had rights. She would have to come home. He had rights. The minivan would have to come home because he had rights and children need their daddies.

"They need their Daddy," he whispered hoarsely, and returned upstairs. Back in bed, he pulled the chain and the night went dark.

***

The alarm woke him at six. He stretched his legs, pushing them straight ahead past the foot of the bed to wake up every muscle and sinew and tendon. He hated the arrival of this time of year. There was no light in the morning. No light and no stars and no moon. Just pre-dawn blackness.

Quietly, he got out of bed and tiptoed into the bathroom. He took a quick shower, and shaved before brushing and flossing his teeth to make sure the nighttime plaque couldn't build up. He tiptoed on into the walk-in closet, where he put on fresh boxers, a white tee-shirt and black socks, followed by the sky-blue dress shirt with the white collar. He chose a paisley tie because he secretly enjoyed the ribbing he always took from Julia, the one about the relic of the eighties.

He put on a charcoal suit, and his favorite black wingtips, and tiptoed back through the master bedroom, not risking a glance at the bed because then he might wake her to make up the fun way and he didn't have time.

He was behind on the big loan to First Merchants, so he grabbed a cereal bar from the pantry and headed directly out the front door. On the porch he stopped when the motion detectors did their jobs, bathing him in white light. He really should pay that damned power bill, he thought. Pay it online and just get it over with.

He went back inside and grabbed the power company envelope. He considered opening the big one from State Farm, but he didn't have time, and besides, the premiums had probably gone up and they were killing a million more freaking trees just to give customers the bad news. The bastards. What a freaking racket.

He was at work by seven, beating the outer-belt traffic before the rest of the suckers were even out of bed. He opened his email, and sent a quick message to Sheila to please put the call through if his wife called, but otherwise he needed to work on the First Merchants loan and should not be disturbed.

One quick trip to the coffee station and he would be in good shape for a productive day. He considered leaving a quick voicemail at home that he'd be happy to do the soccer carpool tonight. Especially if it meant she would shut up with that nonsense about doing it all herself. But the lesson of being realistic, the cornerstone of banking after all, was that one should not promise what one cannot deliver. Julia could do the carpool.

Sheila would put the call through if Julia needed his help. Hell, the Hinmans ought to be able to do it. Maybe just this once, just this *once*, they could be real neighbors.

"When hippos fly," he muttered, and opened the First Merchants file, certain that if he could close the loan by four he could call Julia and let her off the hook.

He had been meaning to video the kids at soccer anyway. Like the Kodak commercials used to ask with that old Paul Anka song…how did that damned thing go anyway? Do you remember…something like that…*do you remember, baby? Do you remember the times of your life?*

Something like that. Cool song, kind of sentimental, and he found Year Four on the amortization schedule, because problems were made for solutions, and solutions were made for problems, and round and round we go.

"Round and round we go," Charley Tolliver whispered, and stood up to go make the morning coffee.

THE INTERRUPTION OF THOMAS DARROW

✳ ✳ ✳

The setting of "The Interruption of Thomas Darrow" is the July 1865 execution of the co-conspirators in the Lincoln assassination. One of the doomed prisoners, Mary Surratt, was the first woman to be executed by the United States government. She was most likely innocent. This story was first published in 2003 by Civil War Camp Chest.

Private Thomas Darrow employed his moist blue uniform sleeves—right, then left, then right again—to mop sweat from his forehead and dripping nose; then he applied the heels of his palms to mat and smooth his quilly red beard, which itched incessantly in the summer heat. Indeed the setting was muggy, but of course it was July and he had borne heat of far greater discomfort than this. He repeated the matting for the third time in the past minute, and pondered whether his doing so was to mask on the one hand, or to signal on the other, his agitation at Delahanty's endless chattering about the damned woman.

From his perch upon the wall, he glanced back at the crowd behind him on the ground twenty feet below. The faces of the ticketless slobs offended Private Darrow with their eager, morbid hunger for any shred of news about the prisoners. For God's sake, he thought, go *home*. It's just a hanging, he was about to mutter to himself, but of course it was not just a hanging, and his attention regrettably returned to the gibberish spewing from Delahanty's tobacco-drenched mouth.

"—all kinda things in my time, but a *woman!* How d'ya hang a *woman?* Tommy, y'ever seen such a thing? A *woman?*"

The stench of Delahanty's breath was powerful in the oppressive heat.

"Back up, Jack. I can hear you."

Delahanty retreated a half-step, and pointed down at the proceedings before them in the shipyard.

"Tommy, we're bout to see a woman hang. Ain't that bother ya?"

Private Darrow stroked his beard thoughtfully, then matted it forcefully again in agitation. When he spoke, he didn't look at Delahanty.

"The president's dead. Someone's got to pay. Just…just because she's a woman doesn't mean she gets special privileges. Remember what the major said this morning. The wheels of justice must turn, and turn they shall. Remember that's what he said."

"But a *woman*, Tommy," whispered Delahanty, gripping Private Darrow's right arm.

Darrow ripped his arm away and turned to glare down at the little nuisance.

"Listen, Jack, and listen good. I'm tired, all worn out, from your futile ramblings about this woman. I'm not wanting to see it either, but it's not as if she's the Virgin Mary." He paused to look without expression at the four gallows standing in wooden unison below. "Just unlucky is all."

"Ha! Unlucky! Tommy, you got a lot more education than me, but I gotta tell ya, *unlucky* ain't the word. Major Highsmith says she didn't have nothin' to do with it. Yeah, maybe Booth and them others would come to her house, but maybe she didn't know nothin' bout killin' the—"

Private Darrow wheeled and cuffed Delahanty by the ear, not letting go. He ignored the putrid tobacco odor and peered into the little soldier's eyes from a distance of not more than five inches.

"I *know* all about it, Jack. I don't need you to be my newspaper. Got it?"

Delahanty appeared to get it, and shrank frailly until Darrow released his ear. Delahanty rubbed the ear with delicate care. "Sorry, Tommy. Jesus. Get no sleep last night?"

Darrow didn't answer. A hush had fallen over the soldiers lining the wall and populating the yard below. A voice on the wall five or six soldiers to Darrow's right hissed to the crowd outside the wall: "The conspirators! They're comin' out soon! God save us all!" Darrow strained to see who this announcer was. Recognizing the speaker, Darrow shook his head faintly. It was George Fann, the Bible-quoting corporal from western Pennsylvania. This didn't surprise Private Darrow, as he despised Corporal Fann's obnoxious, loud piety. It had never seemed to Darrow, in the five months since first meeting the inebriated Fann in the saloon on Water Street, that Fann's actions fit his stated beliefs. He had told Fann precisely such on several sober occasions, but Fann had dismissed Darrow's observations as excessive worry about nothing. Fann had gushed that there was nothing more believable than inconsistency, and Darrow had thrown up his hands and left it to one of the others to try talking sense to the lush.

A man in the crowd yelled, "The Surratt woman? She comin' out?"

Fann hissed back, "Soon! The door ain't opened yet! But no clemency's what we hear!" This revelation drew speculative conversation among the crowd of people who would hear, but not witness, the abrupt termination of four lives on the condemned side of the wall.

Darrow stared at the door through which the prisoners would eventually emerge. He wondered whether she would enter the yard first...indeed it would fit the warped sense of propriety and honor which these damned Lincolnite hypocrites exhibited every single day of their lives. Women first, he thought. At least in the South they meant it, only for the good things. But here in Washington they get it wrong all the time. Through doors, onto carriages, yes, that was fine, but now even to the gallows, now that Stanton and his minions would have their way.

Goddamned son of a bitch Stanton. He's eliminating everyone he knows about, Darrow mused. For weeks Darrow had wondered, sometimes in curiosity and sometimes in desperate fear, what happened to Booth's diary. Everyone knew he kept one, and fanatically at that. So what ever happened to the goddamned thing? He didn't think his own name would be there, but knowing Booth and his attraction to posterity, well, …

"Tommy!" exclaimed Delahanty, poking Darrow's arm. "They're comin' out!"

The door in the sundrenched wall was open. It was so goddamned *hot*. Darrow's heart began to pound, even in his teeth.

Apparently there were final farewells being finished emotionally, as wails of lamentation assailed Darrow's consciousness through the portals of his ears. And then there was movement.

Indeed Mrs. Surratt emerged first from the dark hell of the penitentiary, flanked and seemingly held up by two priests, who in turn were escorted by a blue-coated soldier. As soon as she became illuminated by the July sun, Mrs. Surratt appeared to faint, her fall interrupted by the support from the two priests.

Atzerodt was next out the door, shuffling along in unnecessary shackles, unnecessary due to the armed soldiers hustling him along.

David Herold made a poor accounting of himself, sobbing and teetering as he was pushed out the door by cursing soldiers. What a pathetic exit, Darrow judged.

And then out marched Lewis Paine. Square shoulders, chin up, barefoot as if saying that his natural state was bravery, that it was his natural state he would take with him into eternity.

His natural state. The idea of Paine strangely roiled Darrow's stomach. It always had. His Spartan attitude and total commitment to cause, without ambiguity, had seemed stupid, dense, stone-cold to others. But to Darrow, Paine was the epitome, damn it all to hell, of dedication. Dedication without selfishness. And this combination in Paine had cost Darrow many hours of sleep in the past several weeks.

A straw hat was atop Paine's head. Most of the soldiers on the wall tittered in mocking amusement, as clearly had been the goal of the individual who had placed the sailor's straw on the proud condemned killer's pate.

Of course, Lincoln was the one who had deserved to die. Darrow wasn't opposed to the deaths of those who deserved it, and the Invader-Tyrant surely qualified. But Mrs. Surratt? Perhaps Paine deserved to die for being inept enough to botch the job on the old man Seward (and Booth had said Paine was a born killer!), and then having the colossal brain hemmorhage to not get out of Washington while the getting was good.

And Atzerodt...well, there was a waste of Earth's oxygen anyway. Darrow had long been convinced that Atzerodt was around for just two reasons: Booth liked to surround himself with lesser men (and hence Darrow had committed himself to the mission itself far more than to the man), and assigning Atzerodt to Vice President Johnson was a superior method of implicating Johnson himself in the plot, since there was no chance of Atzerodt actually going through with it. Two birds with one stone, in that event. Lincoln dies; Seward dies; Johnson is implicated in the newspapers by his mere survival and by Booth's note to Johnson at the hotel; Johnson is hence limited to the weakest possible presidency for four years while the South reconstructs itself. As much as Darrow despised Booth and his cocky ego, the plan had been a sound one, if only it had been carried off with the efficiency Darrow himself had shown in getting that idiot Metropolitan guard Parker away from the president.

The problem, to Darrow's regret, was not Booth's death. His survival would have bordered upon miraculous. The problem was in Paine's failure to kill Seward and get away. Without Paine on the gallows, they could never hang Mrs. Surratt today. They could never hang David Herold. They could never hang Atzerodt. Paine was the only person in captivity who had committed violence toward the President's cabinet on that fateful April night. There could be no second, third and fourth noose without Paine's drenched white noose in the summer sun. Booth's error, in retrospect, was in not ensuring that Herold would get Paine out of Washington. Abandoning Paine was a mistake of enormous proportion, and Darrow resented the mistake with every ounce of his will.

Because of that mistake, Darrow found himself staring down at four fresh open graves on a brutally hot summer morning, aware of the fact that among the throng of soldiers and government officials about to witness the murder of an innocent woman on this horrible day, only Lewis Paine, David Herold, George Atzerodt, George Fann, Mary Surratt and Private Thomas Darrow knew that Mrs. Surratt, due in minutes to be the first woman ever executed in the United States, was innocent of the crime of conspiring to assassinate Abraham Lincoln.

And Private Thomas Darrow believed in God. Deeply. He and God had three secrets together. God knew that Darrow had lured Parker from his post outside Lincoln's box to the tavern next door to Ford's Theater, where George Fann had proceeded to buy Parker a total of three jolts of whiskey. God had wanted this action from Thomas Darrow, and Darrow had accepted this responsibility proudly. It was why one James Trombley had left Tennessee nine months ago to become one Private Thomas Darrow of Pennsylvania in the first place.

God knew that Thomas Darrow hated the knowledge, despised it, feared it—the knowledge that he could personally end Mrs. Surratt's suffering only by replacing her on the gallows himself.

And God knew that Thomas Darrow was afraid to die young, and that the only greater fear in his heart was that of dying humiliated.

An elbow from Delahanty jerked Darrow from his reverie. A man in white clothing and a white wide-brimmed hat had stepped out of the doorway into the sunlight. He appeared to be beckoning the prisoners and their escorts to trudge the short hot distance to the scaffolding, which so ominously and ignominiously bore four nooses. Above the stark open graves dug into the disgusting humidity, the platform awaited a mindless Spartan warrior, a no-account idiot, an impressionable child, and an innocent middle-aged woman. These four would be sacrificed by a new nation to the termination of the direction of the past. Of all of them, it was the mindless warrior whose sheer sense of dumb honor so frightened Private Darrow. The honesty of Paine's guilt, coupled with Mrs. Surratt's horrific suffering, poured into Darrow's soul like acid as he stood watch with his Federal comrades atop the Penitentiary wall.

The prisoners were positioned behind their respective nooses, their backs to Darrow and the other soldiers lining the high wall. To Darrow's far left, Atzerodt stood still with shoulders slumped. Herold wobbled in place next to Atzerodt. Paine stood like an oak in defiance of the crowd of soldiers in the yard below. Mary Surratt was helped into a chair several feet behind her waiting rope. Absurdly, an umbrella was used to shield the condemned woman from the wicked sun. Darrow pondered the meaning of men protecting a woman from the sun, in the finest tradition of respectful honor toward a lady, and then minutes later the same men tighening a noose around her neck and plunging her to a violent, lonely and humiliating death illuminated by the same uncaring sun. Vaguely, Darrow considered that such duplicitous treatment of a human being might one day become common. Who knew what the reconstructed nation would be like?

Suddenly there was a commotion in the yard below. Paine had uttered something heard only by the men on the scaffold and several soldiers below.

Delahanty nudged Darrow.

"What'd he say, Tommy?" Delahanty whispered.

Before Darrow could answer, Paine yelled into the yard. This time all could hear.

"The woman is INNOCENT!" he cried. "The woman is innocent!"

The man in white, preparing a gray hood for Mary Surratt's head, paused to look at Paine. All activity on the scaffold stopped for a moment. And then the men on the platform resumed their work in binding the prisoners' ankles together to reduce the unsightly convulsions somewhat, as it would not do to have a hanged woman's undergarments visible to the soldiers below.

Darrow stared at the back of Paine's sturdy head as a white cloth was used to join Paine's ankles together. Paine had proudly projected the awful words which had plagued Darrow's sleep for these last weeks. Strange, Darrow thought, that Paine could say those words a hundred times and the woman would still die an unjust death. But were Private Thomas Darrow to utter those same words, the woman would live another thirty years.

He could do it, he thought. He could do it. Just blurt the words. Blurt them and be done with it. Of course, to make the words count he would have to confess his role and complicity in the plot to kill the president. After all, the simple fact that Lincoln would still be alive if Darrow had failed to get Parker away from his post meant that Darrow's role was second only to Booth's. Until the past several weeks, Darrow had been immensely proud of himself, regretting only that history would never know his name. Confounded *history*, he had thought in repeated daydreamings following the assassination. He had *done* something, something truly historic, and history would not note his name nor his actions. He would have to *suffer*, to be *humiliated*, to *die publicly* and *fifty years premature* in order for history to record his great action.

It wasn't fair. Lincoln was already virtually deified by his death. Booth's name would live on in Southern lore, certainly. Paine would be remembered for his stoic bravery, and now, confound it, he would also be remembered for chivalrously attempting to save the woman's life in the minutes before his own end. Even Atzerodt and Herold would be noted by history. If Darrow were to remain silent as he had for these past months, he would live on for an anonymous four or five decades, taking a wife, raising children, safe from suffering and humiliation and premature death. It simply was not fair that a man who was clever enough to escape detection would have to purchase those three awful tickets as price for immortality.

The words filled his lungs, wanting out of their prison within him. "We are the truth," the words said. "Give us life."

The woman is innocent!

He could say those words. He really thought he could. He glanced over at the obnoxious George Fann, who was enjoying the event. Fann was unconcerned with posterity, and equally concerned with his own welfare. Fann would never lose a minute's sleep over the woman's death or his own anonymity in the record of human history. Darrow envied Fann for his inability to consider either the injustice to the woman or the prospect of anonymity in the roll call of those who impacted human events.

Darrow turned his attention back to the stalwart Paine. As if sensing Darrow's gaze, Paine inexplicably turned, his stare traveling determinedly up the wall. His eyes, dark and emotionless, found Darrow's and attacked with the brute, cold force which Paine was reputed to have exhibited on the battlefield.

Paine's stare challenged Darrow in a manner fit for southern honor. The eyes seemed to say "I hold your life in my hands, Thomas. Just as you hold the woman's life in yours. We are each like unto God at this moment. In all of my dumb Spartan honor, I choose to spare your life, comrade, so that you may spare hers by *choosing* to sacrifice your own. Speak now, so that they may believe you. Her noose will become yours, and that is as it should be. Join me, Thomas. Take honor and courage with you into eternity…"

Delahanty tapped Darrow on the elbow, jolting him again from his reverie.

"Tommy? You okay? Whatsa matter? Hey, he really looks like he's lookin' at *you.*"

Darrow did not answer. Paine held his gaze a few seconds longer, and then a gray canvas hood was drawn over the warrior's face and tightened under his chin, leaving him sightless. Yet, even with the hood and Paine's face turned back toward the baking yard below, Darrow could still see those emotionless eyes. He would never escape them.

Moments later, all four condemned were hooded and bound at the ankles and behind the back at the wrists. Two men held Mary Surratt up, as her knees buckled repeatedly.

You can do it, Thomas. Say the words. *Take her place.*

Darrow squeezed both pant legs at the thigh. The nooses were fitted around the four necks below. To his right, Darrow heard George Fann yell something about the doors of Hell opening wide beneath the four graves. Goddamned hypocrite, Darrow thought. Fann's taking it too far.

I'm guilty. I got Parker to go to the tavern with me. I didn't like Booth, but I liked what he wanted to do, and I had been drinking with Parker on several occasions. I had a drink with him. The woman is innocent! Free her! The woman is innocent! I know because I am guilty.

It would take twenty seconds to confess. Another twenty to waive a trial.

Twenty seconds.

The four condemned were positioned, nooses tightened, atop the long trap door.

Twenty seconds. That's all it would take. And just two, even one, to stop this madness.

Darrow drew a breath. It could be done. The difference between cowardice and courage is action, not attitude, not intent, not conscience. *Action.*

He would say the words. He was sure of it now. *The woman is innocent!* It would freeze them. Freeze the proceedings. He would nobly surrender, declare the woman innocent, watch her weep gratefully as he would be led off in shackles. And she would attend his execution, declaring to all who would listen that this condemned man epitomized honor and selflessness and truth and both moral and physical courage. This man Darrow, she would say in her memoirs, was the ultimate example of true manhood.

He would say the words. Proclaim them proudly. *The woman is innocent!* The chroniclers of history would describe the moment in noble language; the masters would paint him standing tall on the wall, tearing away the blue uniform to reveal the brave home gray underneath. And songsters like Stephen Foster would enter his story into musical legend to be sung by campfires throughout the South.

Yes, he would say the words...Again he drew in a breath.

"THE WOMAN IS INNOCENT!"

Darrow looked around in horror. Had he really said them? The words, though muffled, had been heard clearly throughout the yard below and atop the wall. But they were ignored by the throng of humanity which had grown tired of hearing them. The signal was given anyway by the man in the white clothing and hat. The long trap door swung down and open violently, and the four souls fell.

Long after the twitching of the other three bodies had subsided, Lewis Paine still struggled at the end of his rope. Tears welled in Darrow's eyes. Paine had robbed him.

He had been about to say the words. Paine had rushed to say them first, and now Paine battled at the end of his rope, neck unbroken, fighting to the last. It was entirely unfair. Darrow had been about to say the words. Damn it all to hell, he had been about to say the *words!*

Darrow turned away from the sight of the hooded barefoot body wriggling in the sun.

Facing the crowd outside the wall, he gazed out over the landscape and realized that he had done the right thing by deciding to say the words. He really had *decided*, and that was the important thing. If Paine had not interrupted, the woman would be alive. It was, after all, Paine's second mistake of import. Paine had failed to kill Seward, and now had failed to save Mrs. Surratt by interrupting Private Thomas Darrow.

Later, in the afternoon, Darrow was pensive as he drank several beers with Delahanty. Staring into the golden liquid in his bar mug, he was glad that he had taken the step of deciding. And while fate had caused the interruption by Paine, Darrow resolved now to go forth into his thirties, forties and fifties and eventually make a difference, which he saw now that he was indeed destined to make. After all, he had made one before.

Darrow drained his glass, clapped Delahanty on the shoulder, and strode purposefully out of the tavern and into the teeming street.

A MORNING ALONG THE WAY

✳ ✳ ✳

awn brushed its vague light along Shenita Tabor's eyelids with just a suggestion that she forgot to set her alarm.

Shenita's eyes flung open. It was the first day of school. Day One of her senior year. She *would* go to college. She would *go* to college. After all, her big brother didn't go, and somebody in this family had to pay attention to better things. But first she had to shower, dress and eat breakfast.

Mama was already gone to the drycleaners. There was a little bit of skim left in the fridge, just enough to make the Life soft and spoonable in the purple bowl she preferred because it wasn't part of a set.

She got to the bus stop with a few minutes to spare, Barry's old backpack clinging to her left elbow with five spiral notebooks and a blue Roller Ball pen hiding at its bottom. As the bus came into view from the south end of St. Helena Street, Shenita risked a glance at one of the boys waiting at the curb. His name was Robinson. She didn't know his last name, but his first name was Robinson and his shirt was tucked in.

She wanted to sit next to Robinson. She wanted to sit next to him on the bus. She wanted to sit next to him in class. She wanted to sit next to him at lunch. If he wasn't on the football team, she wanted to sit next to him on the bus ride home to St. Helena Street. If he *was* on the football team, she wanted to do her homework in the stadium stands and catch a ride with Robinson's carpool after practice.

If she could sit next to him on the bus this morning, she'd know if he was on the football team by the time they got to school. She thought she knew the answer already, because his shirt was tucked in and they weren't even at the metal detectors yet. But sitting next to him she could be sure about the afternoon bus ride. She could be sure.

She needed to be sure.

Robinson looked like he was going to college.

As Robinson stood waiting for the bus to pull up, he spoke to no one, looked at no one. His backpack was actually on his back. It was full. He ignored the two guys behind him who thought something was funny about calling each other the n-word at the beginning of each sentence. Shenita could hear them because she was fifth in line and they were tied for second.

The yellow-and-black school bus slowed in front of them, its stop sign out and red lights flashing. The door folded open. Robinson, first in line, hefted his backpack higher onto his shoulders and prepared to step up.

"Hey, *college* boy! Get your *Obama* ass up them steps so white boy can drive us to school," came the loud instructions from one of the pair behind Robinson. Shenita drew her breath sharply and looked at the back of Robinson's head. He proceeded directly up the steps, apparently not having heard the dreadlocked boy behind him.

Shenita watched Robinson turn left at the top and disappear into the torso of the bus. The driver, a middle-aged white man in a royal blue golf shirt and dirty yellow baseball cap, stared straight ahead, his right hand gripping the handle of the old manual door opener. His knuckles looked as white as Wonder bread.

When Shenita got to the top of the steps, she tried to look casual as her eyes searched for Robinson. She found him quickly, halfway down the aisle on the left. He was seated in an aisle seat, with nobody sitting at the window. The bus was about a third full, with two more stops on the way to school. She couldn't quite make a crowded bus her reason for sitting next to him, and unfortunately the aisle seat across from his was occupied by William Smalls, who lived three houses down from Shenita and wasn't going to go to college because he wanted to work on the shrimp boats like his dad and his uncle.

Robinson wasn't going to work on the shrimp boats. His shirt was still tucked in and his backpack was still full, and he didn't pay any attention to losers who said nigger.

She had two or three more short steps to find an excuse to sit next to him. She decided to be direct, and stopped in front of him.

"Hi, Robinson. Can I sit next to the window?" Shenita smiled and held her backpack in front of her apologetically, like she had no choice in the matter and the backpack really just wanted to sit there.

Robinson looked behind him, and then back at Shenita. Saying nothing, he moved his knees to his right, and Shenita said thank you and shimmied past him and sat down on the window side of Robinson with Barry's old backpack in her lap like a dog.

She couldn't think of anything to say as the bus pulled forward and continued its trek along St. Helena Street. She concentrated so hard on coming up with something that she almost missed his question.

"You're Barry Tabor's kid sister, aren't you?"

He wasn't looking at her, but she wasn't looking at him either so that was fair. She answered while examining the left front seam of the backpack.

"Um, yes. Did, did you know my brother?"

An outburst behind them delayed the response, and then

Robinson reached out with his right hand and touched the seat in front of him, still looking straight ahead.

"Yeah. I knew him. I'm sorry about...everything."

Shenita found another seam to examine. This one had a tear in it, the red canvas separating for several inches along a plastic groove.

"That's okay, Robinson. I'll bet Barry liked you. Were you... friends?" She inserted her right forefinger into the torn section of the backpack, and felt one of the spiral notebooks. She pushed the finger in between the metal spiral of the notebook's spine.

"Kind of. But we didn't really, you know, hang with the same people. Um..."

Shenita listened to Robinson's voice trailing off as if it were hiding behind a tree in back of her. She was sure his voice wanted her to come and look behind that tree.

So she did.

"Tell me what happened, Robinson. I miss my brother. Tell me what happened. Please?" Shenita tried to make her plea both plaintive (a new vocab word last year in Mister Swilling's English class) and coy (a new vocab word also in Mister Swilling's English class).

Neither worked. Silence broke through the riotous cacophony (Swilling) in the rows behind them as Robinson inhaled and slapped his palms on his bookbag, turning to look at Shenita.

"Why do you have to ask that? You think the cops didn't ask that a couple of million times? I'm never telling anybody what happened, even if you *are* Barry's sister." Robinson's voice shook almost imperceptibly (Mr. Swilling would have liked the context here, she thought) as he stumbled through the vowels and consonants of 'sister.'

"Sorry," Shenita said. She wrapped her finger around the metal spine of the spiral notebook and squeezed, not knowing what to say, certain she'd blown it. After all, she already knew what happened. But she didn't know that Robinson actually *knew*. She'd just thought she could earn a little sympathy by asking the question plaintively, and maybe earn a little interest by mixing in some coyness.

"Really, I'm sorry, Robinson. I see it's personal for you too. It's just that, well, when your brother commits, you know, it's, like, hard. I miss him, Robinson. But I know what happened, and I'm okay with it now. It's important to be strong, isn't it?"

Robinson's face was blank.

"I'm going to college," he said.

"I know you are," she said. "So am I. They can't stop us, Robinson. Can they?"

Robinson reacted when someone toward the back yelled an expletive at the driver to get a blanking move on, but then returned his attention to Shenita.

"They stopped Barry. What makes you think they can't stop us?"

"Who stopped Barry? The cops?"

"Hell, no." Barry looked behind him again. "*They* did."

Shenita peered toward the back rows of the bus.

"*Who* did, Robinson?"

"They did. They stopped him. And they want to stop me."

"What in the world are you talking about, Robinson? Barry killed himself."

"Every day, every damn day," Robinson said as if he had not heard her, "they call me Obama Ass. Every day they tell me I'm an uppity Obama-ass nigger and to watch it or they're gonna pop a cap on my head. They tell me that in the hall, in the bathroom, on the bus, in the—"

"Robinson, that was last year! This is the first day of your senior year! And who cares what those guys think?"

Shenita was enjoying the conversation. She hoped the bus driver wouldn't really get a blanking move on. This is what *girlfriends* do, she thought. Encourage. Soothe. Occasionally be plaintive and coy.

Stand by their man.

"Everybody cares what everybody else thinks," Robinson said, continuing to stare directly in front of him. "That's what makes this such a crap ride. Except Barry. He didn't care what anybody else thought. He even wanted to go to Country Day. Did you know that?"

Shenita knew that. She knew that.

"And what did he get for it? He said those rich white people at Country Day told your mom Barry could come if she paid fifty percent of the tuition. Seven grand a year. Your mom told Barry and those rich white people she couldn't afford any seven grand a year from cleaning houses, and those rich white people said well, we think everybody should pay what they can afford, and you can pay seven grand a year and so can everybody else, so nobody pays less than seven grand a year. Nobody. So your brother didn't go there and he stayed here and got called Obama ass every day. Until he lost it one day and hit one of those guys in the face and got popped for it. Suicide my ass." Robinson gripped the seat in front of him and rubbed the vinyl so hard that Shenita could hear the squeak over the rumble of the bus engine.

Shenita turned around to look at the guys in the back, then turned to face Robinson. "But Barry jumped off the Broad River Bridge," she whispered hoarsely. "He couldn't swim."

"*They* killed him."

"*Who?*"

"Those guys in the back."

"*Robinson.* How do you *know?*"

The bus pulled into the Lowcountry High School parking lot as Robinson fingered the seat in front of him one more time and then stood up.

"I gotta go to class. So do you, Shenita."

Shenita took her finger off of the spine of her spiral notebook and withdrew it from the hole in her backpack. She had only been posturing when she used Barry to talk to Robinson, but had not guessed that—

"Hey, *Obama* ass!"

The shout had come from the back. Robinson did not respond, as the bus rolled to a stop and the door unfolded again to present the students with a new day's, a new year's, opportunity.

"Obama ASS!"

Robinson stopped. Shenita stopped right behind him, just as she was about to enter the aisle.

Robinson turned to face the back of the bus. Shenita lowered her head and stared at her backpack. None of the students moved. The driver didn't move.

As Shenita stared at her backpack and the hole in it, the silence on the bus hurt her ears.

Shenita didn't look at Robinson when she asked the question.

"Did he pay attention to them, Robinson?" she whispered.

She felt Robinson staring at them. She felt them staring at Robinson. She felt Robinson paying attention to them. Her throat began to ache.

"Barry paid attention to them, Robinson," she whispered hoarsely. "He died because he paid attention to them, Robinson."

The ache in her throat was getting rounder, bigger.

Robinson turned to face Shenita. "What did you say?"

"You heard me." Shenita climbed up onto the seat, still clutching her backpack, still staring at the hole in the backpack. She drew a deep breath as tears began to well in the reservoir of her bottom eyelids. She did not look away from the hole in her backpack.

Robinson touched her elbow. "What are you doing? Get down, Shenita. Come on. Everybody's watching. Let's just—"

"Hey everybody! You hear them, everybody? You hear THEM? My brother died because he paid attention to THEM!"

For a moment it seemed as if the bus was crumpling, yellow and black like old newspaper, folding into itself, onto her, as Shenita began to cry.

"My brother DIED because he paid attention to them!"

She could hear the roof buckle.

"My BROTHER died because he paid attention to them!"

Someone took her arm and tried to pull her down off the seat. The grip was firm but gentle. It might have been Robinson.

She ripped her arm away. Both of her hands gripped the backpack as she continued to stare at the hole that lived there.

"My brother died because he paid ATTENTION to them!"

She could hear the bus driver yelling something. She could hear someone else yelling something, something, something about Michelle Obama Ass. She could hear someone else, another perceptible else (was it Mr. Swilling?), saying "That's enough now" and another perceptible else saying "Let me through" and the hole in the backpack was as big as a basketball and how could it be as big as a basketball and then—

"MY brother died because he paid attention to them!"

She felt herself being lifted up and then down and then her legs walking without weight on them and how could they do that and I can't fly and neither could my brother and I'm a good girlfriend Robinson and I'm a good sister Barry and I'm a good daughter Mama and this hole is too big it's too big I'm going to fix this hole with that Singer machine Grandmama used to use to fix my socks and my brother died because he paid attention to them and stop calling me michelle obama ass cause even white people don't call me michelle obama ass and barry just wanted them to stop he wanted them to stop and I said don't pay attention to them barry don't pay attention to them cause I can take care of myself and i can stop paying attention to them so you won't have to and you won't have to and i don't need the counselor's office why are we going in there when i just want to be a good *girlfriend.*

***

On the Thursday of the week before Thanksgiving, Mama drove Shenita to school. After school she picked Shenita up and they cleaned the Armstrongs' house together. It was fun because the Armstrongs weren't home and they both got to listen to their iPods.

"Tomorrow we got the Larsons' house," said Mama on the way home. "We get to have as much Gatorade as we want, even if Miss Missy is at home, as long as we change the sheets. All on the same dime, Shenita. Don't much matter what the job is, cause it is."

"Better than nothing, right, Mama?" Shenita smiled into the question.

"Anything's better than nothing, child. That's some wisdom there, sure is."

At home, Shenita turned on the television, but it was three minutes before six, and three minutes before six meant three minutes of commercials, so she pulled her cell phone from her right front pocket and texted a message to one of her friends. She waited, focused on the little screen in her hand, eagerness moving her eyes in darts and flicks.

The response came quickly. She clicked to view it. Then she laughed, punched four buttons to share her laughter, and got up to retrieve the last of last Friday's Gatorades from the door of the refrigerator.

MARCO POLO

✳ ✳ ✳

Please don't take me to Jared's birthday party. *Please.*

I just want to watch Spongebob. Please let me just watch Spongebob and Patrick and Squidward 'cause I don't want to go to Jared's birthday party and I really really *really* don't want Jared's mom and Mary Alfred's mom and Joey's dad to keep staring at me when they think I'm not looking but I am, I *am* looking. *Please Mom I don't want to go. Stop! I don't like that shirt!*

That shirt reminds me of the time the spaghetti fell off my face and Joey laughed and got detention for saying the freaky crip has spaghetti on his shirt to go with the drool. Then Joey kept telling everyone on the playground except Miss Evans that I got him in trouble. *Please,* Mom. I don't want to wear that shirt...

Thank you, Mom. I don't like the shirt, but I'll wear it anyway 'cause I'm glad you remembered to change me down there 'cause I don't like to go when I'm with the other kids even though Miss Evans says they should never call me a baby for wearing a diaper.

Okay. If I have to go to Jared's birthday party and wear this shirt, I hope I got him something cool for a present 'cause if it's not cool Joey will wait till the parents can't hear and he'll tell everyone to look at the lame present the freaky crip gave to Jared and everybody will laugh.

Please, Mom. Let me just watch Spongebob and Patrick and

Squidward 'cause I know the present's gonna be lame 'cause you're not excited enough to show it to me and you must've bought it when I was at therapy yesterday and I wish you'd just *show me*. It's gonna be lame and Joey's...Joey's...If you could just let me watch Spongebob I promise to only go number two, like, once a day.

If I could only go number two once a day, maybe you could stop asking God what you did to deserve this. To deserve me. You know, Mom, if you just let me watch Spongebob and Patrick and Squidward more and you could stop taking me to birthday parties and pool parties and ones that are both like Jared's, then maybe I could maybe go number two just once a day and you could stop asking God what you did when you cry.

Sometimes I ask God what I did, Mom. To deserve me. I promise I would swim at the pool parties, but I did something to deserve me and to make you deserve me but I don't know what I did but I'm sorry I don't remember anything else but *this*. I wish I could swim and run and clean my bottom and make you proud of me and maybe then Dad would come back and you would thank God instead of asking him those questions.

I like this ramp better than the old one. It's not as jerky. Oh, can I have a DVD in the van yet? Can I? I see other kids with them and I promise I can understand the stories in the movies just like I understand Spongebob and I understand you and Miss Evans and Joey and...

I didn't know Jared lived this close, Mom. Who are you talking to? I heard you say we're pulling into the party and it's gonna be good for Todd to be around other kids on a Saturday. You always say that, but Oh God Mom, *please* just let me watch Spongebob and Patrick and Squidward.

Is that Dad on the phone, Mom? It must be. You're pretty mad at whoever that is, and it isn't me so it must be Dad. You would only say *that* to Dad, that thing about shirking responsibilities, and you say that on the phone sometimes when you're taking me somewhere you don't really want to take me. I know that's Dad, Mom, and I know that's his voice mail. I know lots of things, Mom. Like I know that you love me, Mom, and I know that you want to know what God thinks you did to deserve this. I promise I'd go somewhere else, Mom, so you could deserve something different. But you'd have to take me there. I guess that's the pickle you talk about with your friends when you talk about somebody taking Dad's place someday.

I like this new ramp, but not when it's taking me to a birthday party that's a pool party. I wish the ramp would break right now so we'd have to go home and I could see what Spongebob is doing. He's my best friend. Patrick's my second-best friend. Squidward's not always nice but he's my third-best friend.

My friends wouldn't like Joey. They would ask me, *ME*, if Joey should be allowed in Spongebob's pineapple house for my birthday party or Spongebob's or Patrick's birthday party and I'd say no and that would be *IT*. Joey would be out. *OUT*. Just like that. And we'd play in the pineapple and eat crabby patties and run up on the sand sometimes and play with Sandy the squirrel and just have fun being friends and laughing and sometimes crying together and—

They're all here. Except Miss Evans 'cause it's Saturday and she's doing whatever teachers do on Saturday like maybe grading papers or cleaning desks or—

I don't see Joey. I don't see Joey! Quick! Look for his dad. If his dad's not here, this might not be so bad. I don't see Joey's dad! Mom! I don't see Joey's dad! Joey's not here!

Okay. Maybe the food will be good, and it won't fall off the spoon when Mom puts it in my mouth. I'll try real hard when it's cake time to open wide enough to keep the icing off my face. Where's the cake? Oh. We're going right out to the pool?

Do we have to go *right* out to the pool? I always get put under an umbrella like my skin is any different from everybody else's, and they put my wheelchair right where my eyes have to look at everybody swimming.

Who said that? Was that Joey? Please God, don't let it be Joey.

It's Joey. There he is, in his same blue swim trunks with the yellow dolphin on the back. Marco Polo, he says. Let's play Marco Polo, he says. He never said that before. What's Marco Polo? What difference does it make, Mom? You're explaining the game to me and how it works and it will be so much fun to watch and *please can I have some cake and go* **HOME?**

Joey just saw me, Mom. He just *saw* me. And his dad thinks I shouldn't be here because when I'm here kids have to hold back a little when they're supposed to be having fun. Hey! Hear that, Mom? Mom? Did you hear that? Mom? Don't go make sandwiches, Mom! Please don't go make sandwiches. Joey just said maybe Todd should play and everybody sure thought that was funny. Didn't you hear that? I guess Joey's pretty good at saying stuff like that when the grownups are busy making sandwiches and stuff. Like yesterday when Miss Evans and Mrs. Littleford were over in the corner cutting out the cardboard Christmas trees with snow on them even though it never snows in Miami, and Joey said maybe they could cut *Todd* up like a Christmas tree since I move just about as much as a tree. Very funny, I wanted to say, but I guess it really was, 'cause Susan and Jared and Mary Alfred and Juan all thought it was funny and Joey said we'll get our chance and they thought that was funny too.

So the person who's It says Marco with his eyes closed, and everybody is supposed to be honest and say Polo so that maybe It can find them and tag them and make them It. I wish I could tag them and make them It. I really wish I could tag them and make them It. If I could tag them and make them It, then maybe Dad would come home and I wouldn't be It anymore.

There's Joey and he's It. Only his eyes are open and he's cheating and nobody's saying anything about it. They're just letting Joey cheat, and God that's not fair.

Why's he getting out of the water? Joey, don't get out of the water when you're It. Somebody say Joey don't get out of the water when you're It. *Joey, don't get out of the water when you're **IT**!*

MOM! *Hey, I'm not playing Joey, I can't play, Joey! Please! Mom! I can't play Marco Polo!* ***MOM! I CAN'T PLAY MARCO POLO! DAD? DAD! DAAAAAADDY!***

It burns, Daddy. It burns down here. I don't know how to play I don't know how to play I don't know how to   play   I know how to sleep   I know how to

Who lives in a pineapple under the sea? Spongebob? Can I come in? Patrick! Squidward! A crabby patty? For me? I always wanted to live in a pineapple under the sea. Ay, ay, Captain. Look! I can make crabby patties too. Just like you. I'll take that bed over there. If you think that's fair.

Spongebob, did somebody say Pull? No thank you. I'm full. But if I can play...

...I'll be happy to stay.

ABOUT THE AUTHOR

T.D. Johnston's stories have appeared or are forthcoming in *Mulberry Fork Review, Rod Serling Books Presents, Literary Juice, O. Henry, PineStraw Magazine, Hobart Literary Journal, Civil War Camp Chest* and *Short Story America*, among others. "Friday Afternoon," the title story of this collection, is currently under option and in film development in California. His first novel, *Reciprocity*, is due out in 2017. He is currently at work on his second novel, *The Daffodil Society*. A member of the Board of Governors of the South Carolina Academy of Authors, he resides in Beaufort, South Carolina, where he serves as editor of the *Short Story America* anthology series of short fiction.

CPSIA information can be obtained at www.ICGtesting.com
Printed in the USA
LVOW11*1521220616

493668LV00009B/46/P